JONAS BLACKHEART
The 7th Jackal

a novel by J.L. Davis

Dedicated to everyone who wonders if I'm writing about them. I am.

Thanks to Soundcheck Records, Jim Thorpe PA, the last Great independent record store in America.

Special thanks to Annette Sanders Troutman.

Also, Nadine Suchon Schmidt and her partner in crime, Anne Davis Shupp

... and all the rest who are too many to mention (but did anyway inside the book)

"Scared of the dark? You should be. Masterfully written."

The Ink House

Part 1

AGENT LOCKE

1

Alien Country

Hot sun beat down on the Nevada blacktop. Wind in her hair, Special Agent Emma Locke headed north on Highway 93. The abrupt shift of inner-city streets to desert terrain gave her the sensation of being transported to another world.

Emma gassed up the car at a Chevron station. She pondered rumors about travelers from distant worlds that gathered under the bright Nevada sky. It didn't take a conspiracy theorist to put a spin on the legendary road. Ever since Area 51 charted, the desolate tract of land had been a favorite destination for UFO hunters. Welcome to the Extraterrestrial Highway.

Turning left, she passed a huge cottonwood tree. The north gate of Area 51 baked in the rising mid-summer heat. Signs were posted on a barbwire fence that read:

NO UNAUTHORIZED ADMITTANCE, VIOLATORS WILL BE SHOT

The place was surrounded by cameras and floodlights. A soldier stepped out of a guard shack. Emma hit the brakes and held a badge out the window.

Radioing for clearance, he opened the gate.

"That way." The guard pointed. "First building on the east end."

———

In the desert backdrop, radar equipment kept tabs on incoming and outgoing aircraft. Airplane hangars and helicopter ramps were setup on both sides of the road. There was also a fire station, rec center and even a Starbucks with a statue of a little green alien sipping a Frappuccino.

Emma turned into the parking lot of the MARS 1 complex. The building was painted drab gray and ringed with fenced wire. It resembled a maximum-security prison rather than a military outpost.

A guard wearing a gold earring stepped out of the entrance. "Miss Locke?"

Emma nodded.

"Follow me."

Emma's footsteps echoed in the dingy halls of the building. Fluorescent lights illuminated the corridor. One blinked as if ready to burn out. Dull paint on the walls, gray with age, carried the burden of many untold military secrets.

The guard abruptly stopped halfway down the passageway.

"Wait here," he ordered and disappeared down the hall.

2

Cell Number 6

Alone in the corridor, Emma stared at a detainment chamber girded with a steel door. A small window was cut into the metal. She peered inside at a ten-foot windowless cell. The floor, dirty and concrete, had been furnished with a discolored mattress and a stool made of tamperproof material. An overhead camera monitored a wash basin and unscreened toilet.

"Comfortable as a lion's den," she whispered.

A detainee sat stone-still at a small table in the center of the room. Black as oil, his crusty eyes stared blankly at a wall. A ragged scar sullied his left cheekbone. Ankles shackled, his foot tapped anxiously on the cement floor.

Emma heard footsteps coming. She turned to see a man in a long dark suitcoat. Holding a manila envelope, he nodded and smiled.

"Agent Locke? We spoke on the phone earlier. I'm Lanster. Can I call you Emma?" His half-lidded eyes traced down her slim frame.

Emma pulled her coat shut. She glanced at the floor before meeting his gaze. "Agent Locke will be fine."

Lanster raised his jaw and stiffened at the woman's cold approach.

Emma looked at the cell door. "Who is he?"

"His name is Jonas Blackheart," said Lanster.

For an instant the prisoner lifted his head and glared.

"He looks feral," she said.

"Feral isn't the word. Blackheart has a resume longer than the state of California. He once shot a cashier and a hostage at a convenience store, just to teach the cops a lesson." Lanster's droopy eyes, weighty buckets of wet sand, again rolled down Emma's slender build.

Emma's shoes shifted nervously on the floor.

Early thirties, most of her friends were housewives attending PTA meetings. Instead, sometime after college she applied for a position at the CIA. An interview and polygraph later, she entered a rigorous training program. She got assigned to an office in Washington. The job was simple; monitor caseloads of suspected felons and drug lords on the hitlist. Not exactly storming a terrorist camp in Kabul but it had its moments.

The call from headquarters came unexpectedly. A VIP in the head office told her to report to Area 51. The following morning, she boarded a jet from Dulles International. After a long desert drive up the Extraterrestrial Highway, she pulled into the most controversial military base in the United States.

"I haven't been debriefed. What's this all about?" she asked Lanster.

"Maybe you better see for yourself."

Lanster nodded at a security guard who unlocked the cell door.

Stiff as nails, Emma stepped forward.

"Wait." Lanster grabbed her arm. "Check your weapon."

"Excuse me?"

"No guns, knives or anything else hidden in a sock. No offense. You could get unnerved. Heavy on the trigger. We can't afford any slipups."

Hesitating, Emma set her Glock on a table. "Satisfied?"

An authoritative grin washed over Lanster.

Followed by Lanster and two guards with batons, Emma stepped in the room, shoes clicking against stone flooring.

Jonas Blackheart sat at a wooden table, fingers steepled in front of him.

"There's no restraints on his wrists," Emma noted.

"Trust me," Lanster said. "Handcuffs won't do any good here."

3

Behind the Iron Curtain

Lanster walked over to the prisoner and snapped his fingers in his face. "Jonas? You got a visitor. You gonna play nice?"

Jonas's savage eyes narrowed. Heavy breathing echoed against stone walls.

Emma tightened her fists and stepped closer. A long scar cut down the side of the prisoner's cheek. A deep blemish, perhaps an old bullet wound, marred his neck.

"What has he been into?" she asked.

"More than selling music in the local record shop." Lanster walked around the table. "He had a few run-ins with the wrong people. The last time nearly killed him. One of our sister agencies found him on a mountainside, busted up like a jackhammer on cement. He should be dead. We managed to revive him." Lanster bent down and looked closely at the prisoner. "Do you hear me Jonas? Wake the hell up."

Jonas shifted his weight uneasily. The guards instantly raised their nightsticks. Lanster held up a hand and ordered them to stand down.

"I read his M.O.," Emma said. "The case file didn't reveal much. Said he killed two people at a convenience store. That doesn't pay for room and board at Area 51."

"It isn't what he did," said Lanster. "It's what he can do." He uncrossed his arms and pulled out a chair, opposite the prisoner. "Sit down. Don't make any sudden moves. The last thing we wanna do is piss him off."

Emma cautiously lowered herself on the chair. Jonas remained silent. His cold eyes, dark rivers in winter, hardened on her.

"What now?" she asked.

"You're the profiler. You'll figure it out."

Grinning, Lanster motioned the guards towards the exit.

Emma tilted her head in confusion. "Where are you going? Lanster!"

Guards tracing after him, Lanster walked out and slammed the cell door shut.

Everything grew quiet. Everything except the heavy breathing of the man sitting on the other side of the table. Biting down on her lip, Emma turned around.

4
Jonas Blackheart

Jonas glared. His face was pale. Almost drab. He clearly hadn't been exposed to sunlight for a long time.

Emma steadied her trembling hands.

"Jonas Blackheart, can you hear me?" she asked.

Grimy sweat streaked the side of the prisoner's neck. Metal shackles on his ankles rattled when he suddenly moved.

Emma instinctively reached for her Glock but stopped. The gun sat on a table outside the cell.

"Lanster!" she shouted again. "Open the goddamn door!"

Jonas's lips pulled up in a sadistic grin. Settling back in his chair, he laughed darkly. Its haunting presence reverberated through the confines of the small cell.

Emma raised her badge. "My name is..."

"I know what your name is," Jonas cut her off. "CIA, right?" He studied her closely. Saliva dripped from the corner of his mouth. "You don't fit the bill of an operative. Too soft around the eyes."

Emma's fingernails dug into her palms. "You underestimate me."

"Do I?" Jonas laughed again. His stained molars, brown with corruption, opened wide. Emma couldn't help picturing an alligator waiting on dinner. "Tell me something Dick Tracey. You don't look stupid. Probably went to college. Studied hard between frat parties and midnight panty raids at the dorm. What made a girl like you join Intelligence?"

Emma stared, refusing to flinch.

Blackheart was smart. Savvy. People made the mistake of viewing killers as unintelligent. Not true. The Unabomber had a genius IQ. Bundy was no slouch either. Underestimating Blackheart wouldn't only be a mistake. It could prove deadly.

"I'll ask the questions." Emma scanned the drab cellblock. A large spider, black and yellow, hung from a cobweb on the wall. "The military doesn't lock prisoners in dungeons in the middle of the Nevada desert for murdering two people with a shotgun. What are you doing here?"

"You first," countered Jonas. "A woman like you? You should be home. Pregnant. Maybe in flipflops on a beach. Instead your trying to save the world. Isn't that right Agent Locke?"

"I told you," she said. "I ask the questions. Get used to it."

There was a frozen moment of silence, thick as mud. Emma got up and walked towards the door.

"I'll be back. We'll talk more later." She knocked on the cell door for the guards.

Jonas grinned. After a moment, "It was a hot July night, wasn't it?"

Emma stopped cold. She turned around. "What did you say?"

"Don't play stupid." He shifted forward in his chair, fingers folded. "That was the day your life turned down a dark road, wasn't it?"

A disturbing glow flickered in Emma's damp face. "You don't know what you're talking about."

Jonas stared brutally. A droplet of sweat dripped off his cheek. "Don't treat me like a fool, Agent Locke. Answer me!" He slammed a fist on the table.

Emma flinched. Turning around, she knocked harder on the exit door. "Lanster? Open up!"

A sudden gush of heat penetrated the back of Emma's neck, almost as if the sun peaked out from behind thick white clouds. The room temperature became hot. Oppressive. She grew lightheaded. Things moved slower. She gripped the wall for support.

Jonas's gaze remained fixed. Concentrated. "Can you feel it Agent Locke? Can you feel it deep down in your bones? Time to go down the rabbit hole."

Emma's knees buckled and she blacked out on the floor.

5
In the lap of a Dream

It was dark. A dead calm. Emma saw shadows. Heard voices. The world grew hazy as a dream but real as a human touch.

Clump, clump, clump.

Heavy footsteps.

"Don't say a word," Emma whispered. She held her sister tight. Blanket pulled over their heads, someone walked towards them.

Clump, clump, clump.

Maddy shivered. She reached up. Put her arms around Emma and head against her. Tears splashed her neck.

"I'm scared sis." Maddy's voice cracked with terror. "I'm scared deep down in the bones."

Clump, clump, clump.

Emma peeked out the door. Tension, thick as fog after a drenching rain, clouded the air. Window curtains flapped in a warm breeze. Pale moonlight illuminated a darkened silhouette standing in the doorway.

"Don't leave me sis," Maddy cried, her voice disappearing into an echo.

Clump, clump, clump.

This time the noise was different. Muffled, like someone plodding down old rickety steps. Then silence. Dead silence.

One second. Two seconds. Three and then...

BOOM!!

6

Waking Moments

Emma opened her eyes and bolted straight up.

"Can you hear me? Agent Locke?" Lanster snapped his fingers in her face.

Emma looked around. "Where am I?"

"You're in my office," said Lanster. "Safe."

Emma rubbed knuckles in her eyes. The last thing she remembered was talking to Jonas Blackheart. Then everything went blank. She had a terrible dream. God, it was vivid. Sharp as an arrow dipped in blood. Memories flowed of that terrible night with Maddy. Somehow Blackheart reached inside her mind. Pulled out her darkest fears.

"How did I get here?" she asked.

Lanster said, "You blacked out. We found you on the floor. What happened in there?"

Emma stared ahead. Vivid as a train wreck, she swore she was seventeen again, reliving an old nightmare. Telling Lanster would get her dismissed from the case. She'd be labeled delusional.

"Nothing." Emma looked down at her shoes.

"You're lying."

"I said nothing," she answered sternly and picked up a glass of water. Hands shaking, she took a sip and set it back down.

"Tell me what's going on here Lanster. Jonas Blackheart. Who is he?"

"The better question is what he is," said Lanster. "He has a way of drilling into people's skulls."

Someone knocked on the door. Lanster opened it. A man in his mid-thirties walked in. Emma recognized him immediately. In Washington, he had the brand of being a legend. Drug cartels. Terrorists. He tangled with the bad element from coast to coast.

"This is Jason Diggs," said Lanster.

Smiling, he took Emma's hand and squeezed it gently. "My pleasure."

"I've heard your name," said Emma. "Some of your work was case studies back at the academy."

Diggs shrugged. "Not as exciting as it sounds. My toughest job was learning to change diapers for my kids after I got divorced."

Emma smiled. Diggs had a boyish charm. No doubt a killer with the ladies.

"I haven't been given much information," she said. "Judging by where we are, it's more than unpaid parking tickets."

"Area 51, right?" Diggs waved his finger in a circle. "Take it from me. You've only begun to see the tip of the universe."

———

Diggs pushed the door shut. Walking around the room, he sat down on the edge of a table. Emma's eyes gave him the once over. He was a handsome man. Dark wavy hair. Playful blue eyes. By the way he tilted his head and lifted his eyebrows, a bit of a flirt.

"My guess is you've got a million questions," said Diggs.

"It isn't every day you get flown off to the Nevada desert."

Diggs smiled. "Don't get it wrong. This isn't about dissecting little green men nor is Jonas Blackheart your typical assassin."

Emma tilted her head questionably. "I read his file. He disappeared off the grid after going on a killing spree. He's listed as deceased. Some kind of traffic accident."

Diggs crossed his legs and folded his hands. "Reports of Blackheart's demise are overstated. His case is classified. The CIA used to have a sister bureau called The Agency. Blackheart had dealings with them. You might say he was their masterpiece. He wanted out of the organization. People don't quit in our business, at least the ones with top secret info at their fingertips."

Emma raised an eyebrow. "What information?"

"Things," Diggs answered evasively. "You'll find out soon enough. The point is that Blackheart felt his life was in danger. He disappeared off the network. When the Agency finally caught up to him, he was found in the woods full of bullet holes. Headquarters didn't want the police prying open his life so they faked his death.

"The CIA took over his case after the Agency closed up shop a few years back. We put Jonas in a maximum-security prison in Tulsa. Let's just say he didn't play nice with other prisoners. He broke a prisoner's neck for refusing to give him a cigarette. The decision was made to have him flown to Area 51. He's been locked up here in a padded cell ever since."

Emma eyed Diggs closely. He was your typical spy; lots of

data but dodged all the questions.

Diggs stood up and walked over to Lanster who handed him a file. He opened it and paged through the papers. "I read your profile Emma. You scored high in psychology." Slapping the folder shut, he tossed it on the table. "What we need from you is to stick close to Jonas Blackheart. See what makes him tick. What you should know is that he's one hell of a brilliant manipulator. You're green around the ears. He'll use that to his advantage. He'll try to get inside your head. Don't let him." He stepped to the door. "Any other questions?"

Emma blinked uncertainly. "I don't get it. You said it yourself. I don't have any field experience. We're in Area 51. That's the most secretive military base in the country. The case has to be huge. Why would headquarters pick me?"

Diggs hesitated. "We didn't," he said. "Jonas Blackheart requested you."

7
Pictures from long Ago

Emma's quarters were a mile down the road from the MARS building where Jonas Blackheart was interred.

Seated at a desk in her room, she reached in her purse and pulled out a picture of Maddy, her sister. She carried it all these years. Maddy sat on a set of swings in the backyard. Curly brown hair draped her shoulders. The photo had been taken just days before the incident that changed her life forever.

Swallowing hard, Emma set the picture down and opened her laptop.

One of the CIA's databanks indicated that Blackheart attended the University of Pittsburgh. He majored in phycology and held a 3.0 grade average. Then his world suddenly shifted. Jonas quit college and went off the radar for months. When he finally resurfaced, he turned up at a convenience store with a shotgun and an attitude. Little to no other information existed. As far as Emma could determine, he'd been rotting away in cell number 6 ever since.

———

Emma's cell phone rang. Picking it up off the dresser, she hit the talk button.

"Hello?"

"Emma? It's Jason Diggs. Just checking in." He paused. "Lanster told me that you fainted in Blackheart's cell today. What happened?"

More like transported back in time to relive a nightmare, Emma thought. Blackheart somehow hypnotized her.

"It was a long flight. Jetlag," she lied.

Diggs got silent. No doubt he knew about her past. The CIA subjected her to a battery of tests to evaluate her mental state. Headquarters determined that rather than crack like an egg, her tainted youth thickened her skin.

Emma changed gears. "I still have a few questions."

Diggs laughed. "Only a few? Fire away."

"You said Jonas Blackheart requested me. Why would he do that?"

The phone got quiet again.

"Hard to say," Diggs answered. "Blackheart sees television. Sometimes he bribes guards for newspapers. Maybe he saw your name someplace. You have a colorful history. Damn shame what happened," he said quietly. "As for Jonas Blackheart, you'll just need to trust me. He's a different kind of animal. Depending on your viewpoint, you might even say he's the most dangerous person in the world. He's also the only one who can save it."

Emma opened her mouth and closed it. Diggs was being evasive again.

"Get some sleep," he said. "It'll be a long day tomorrow. I'll meet you back at the MARS building in the morning. You'll be debriefed. Fair enough?"

"Sounds like a plan," said Emma.

"Remember. Blackheart isn't just smart. He's dangerous."

"Understood."

Diggs hesitated. "I'm not sure you do, but you will."

8

MARS

Emma pulled into the MARS building the next morning. Set in deep blue, brilliant sun baked the badlands. Sipping at a Starbucks, she yawned tiredly. Encounters with Jonas Blackheart left her spooked.

The front door of the MARS building opened. A guard with a five-o'clock shadow stepped out. Motioning her forward, he led Emma into the building and down a long corridor. At the end of the hall, he pointed left towards Lanster's office.

"That way," he directed.

Emma knocked and walked in. Lanster sat behind a big oak desk, drinking coffee and rummaging through files. He swung around in his leather chair. His gaze hung on her shapely curves like an iron weight.

No doubt about it. Lanster was a womanizer, not to mention a narcissist. He tapped his fingers on the gold nameplate sitting on the corner of his desk as if to let her know who was in charge.

He pointed at the coffee pot and pastry tray. "Morning. Coffee and donuts are on the house."

Emma forced a smile. "No thanks," she declined. "I did some research last night. There weren't many records available on Jonas Blackheart. In fact, he's supposed to be dead."

"You know the CIA. Only believe half the things you see or hear. His death has been exaggerated," said Lanster.

"You mean faked," she countered. "Not even Manson got a guest suite in Area 51. What makes him so unsafe?"

Lanster stood up. Draining the last of his coffee, he stepped towards the door. "The best person to answer that question is Jonas Blackheart."

———

Lanster led Emma down the hall to cell number 6. Peeking in the door's porthole, things appeared quiet.

"It's like before. Keep your distance," said Lanster. "He isn't medicated. That makes him more dangerous but you got better things to do than talk to a zombie."

"Is he secure?"

Lanster smirked. "You still don't get it, do you? Shackles aren't the problem. Our boy has other weapons at his disposal."

Nodding at a guard, the cell door opened. Lanster started to walk in.

"Wait," Emma said. "We don't need him spooked. Maybe I should go alone."

Lanster drew back in surprise. "That's brave as hell, Agent Locke. Stupid, but brave. Make no mistake. The only spook here is Jonas Blackheart."

Emma raised her jaw, trying to appear confident. Other than the frightening experience she had the last time they met, she had no idea what Blackheart was capable of. Still, if she wanted his trust and respect, she'd need to portray strength. A woman surrounded by guards didn't paint a picture of self-assurance.

"Please." She tilted her head and offered a smile.

Uncrossing his arms, Lanster nodded. "Have it your way. I never get too close anyway. The last thing I need is that bastard getting in my head. There's an emergency button installed under the interrogation table. If things get dicey, push it. We'll be outside the door."

Emma set her Glock on the table. After a moment, she walked in.

9
The Dead Man in Cell Number 6

The heavy steel door slammed shut behind Emma.

Jonas sat quietly at the grilling table, legs chained. His eyes were black stones on a windless beach. Heavy breathing echoed in cadence. After a minute he looked up and cracked a dark smile.

"Didn't you have enough last time, Agent Locke?" he asked smartly.

Emma remained stock-still, resisting the temptation to turn around. "I have a few questions."

"Of course. CIA agents can never suck enough blood. They're leeches."

Stepping forward, Emma sat down in the chair opposite Jonas. She glanced down at his hands. They were huge. Almost abnormal. He tapped a knuckle evenly on the wooden tabletop.

Smiling greenly, he said, "So how can you entertain me today?'

"You tell me," said Emma. "You requested me to come here. Why?"

Jonas stopped tapping and folded his hands. "I thought Intelligence had all the answers. Don't get the wrong idea. You're not here because you're brilliant. In the end, you're nothing but a rookie CIA agent wondering how she's going to get out of here alive, isn't that right?"

Emma held a firm gaze. She couldn't back down. Blackheart would see the weakness. Feed on it.

"You can't intimidate me," she told him.

"Is that so?" Jonas laughed. He unexpectedly jerked his lumbering body forward. Emma jumped. She immediately drew her hand to the security button underneath the table. Jonas settled back again. A smirk painted his lips.

"You see, Agent Locke? You're not a professional. You're not even a good liar. You should be honored that I gave you the opportunity to be here."

"You're a killer," she reminded. "You think that deserves admiration?"

"I have a few rough edges. Still I know how to treat a woman. Take a man like Lanster." He glanced up at the security camera. "He's watching us. Bastards like that have x-ray vision. Can you feel his eyes crawling on your skin? He wants you, you know. He'd love to rip the buttons off that cheap white blouse you're wearing. Throw you down on the cold cement. Make you moan like a whore." Jonas exhaled deeply. "That's not me. My passions run deeper than a wet night under the sheets."

Emma tilted her head. "You think I'm naïve?"

"No," he said flatly. "I think you're subpar."

"Intelligence trusted me enough to come here. That's hardly subpar."

Jonas leaned back in his chair. An amused grin danced across his lips. "Don't flatter yourself. You're here because I want it that way. Make no mistake, Agent Locke. You're no rising star in the espionage world." He shifted forward and added, "But you could be by the time this is over, at least if you're not dead."

Emma stared. Blackheart was clever. The mid-morning sun hadn't hit and already he tried to get into her head. Twist her thoughts. She was tempted to ask him about what happened on her last visit when she blacked out but refrained. He wouldn't answer the question anyway. She needed more time to weed him out. Opening a file, Emma paged through some papers.

"You attended the University of Pittsburgh," said Emma. "An honor student. Suddenly you dropped out. Disappeared. A few months later you walked into a convenience store and shot two people in cold blood." She closed the file and slid it halfway across the table. "How does a guy who never even got a parking ticket suddenly decide to go on a killing spree? Did something snap?"

Jonas rubbed his chin thoughtfully as if considering. "Trust me. People are capable of anything. It just takes a determined attitude and the right number of bullets."

Emma paused. He was trying to dig under skin. Piss her off. Make her stand up and storm out the door. Stiffening her jaw, she held firm.

"You worked for the government," she continued. "An organization called The Agency. Tell me about it."

Flickers of tension chalked Jonas's expression but quickly dissolved. "That was a fun bunch. One in particular, Harry Grimm, took a special interest in me."

Emma scribbled his name down on a notepad.

"Don't bother," said Jonas. "Grimm is dead. In fact, I killed him. Just another ghost in my little chest of dreams."

A satisfied shadow crossed his lips. It was the look of a

Doberman who shredded a rabbit and carried it away proudly in its jaws like a trophy.

Emma stopped writing and looked at Jonas. She couldn't help but to notice that something was gone in his eyes. God knows what goes on in a killer's mind. People like Dahmer cannibalized his victims. Kept the bones as medals of honor. Jonas Blackheart didn't remind her of a flesh-eater. He had a rational side. Derived pleasure from toying with people's thoughts. Once he finished, he'd kill his victims or if luck had it, drive them to suicide.

Smiling, Jonas's teeth were brown; broken icicles in a cesspool. "You think I'm a monster," he said. "Nothing could be further from the truth. I'm just a misunderstood victim."

"Everyone on death row is," Emma reminded. "Just ask them."

Jonas wagged a finger. "Clever girl."

"I'm not trying to be clever. I'm trying to get to the truth." Emma's demeanor remained solid as a brick.

Jonas laughed out loud but his stare turned suddenly to stone. He slammed a fist on the table. "Don't talk to me like I'm a child, Agent Locke. You're here to exorcise ghosts. You know what ghosts are, don't you? Apparitions. Demons from the past that won't go away. Tell me," he prodded. "Something happened to you long ago. Something too terrible to remember. You feel responsible. Never forgave yourself. Guilt. It's like maggots on dry bones. People get eaten up by it."

Emma pulled at the fleshy part of her hand.

"That's smart but we're not here to talk about my life. I need to know about yours." She looked around the drab cell. "My guess is you've been here for a long time. Maybe I could change that."

Amusement sprinkled Jonas's expression. "Haven't you forgotten something? I brought you here. I make the rules," he said. "Tell me more about that terrible night long ago. Your life became isolated. You wanted to find that special someone. Maybe a passionate soul to make wild lust to on a stormy night. But you just couldn't allow yourself happiness, could you? Guilt again. The elephant in the room. Instead of living the American dream, you joined the CIA. You thought that just maybe if you could save someone else's life, you'd make restitution for the past. Erase those awful visions and the smell of gun powder in the air."

Emma glared. "You don't know anything about me."

Jonas mused. "Really? I know people died that night. I also know you were adopted. You're an outsider. A bastard child. Your real parents disappeared. Many a night you lay awake wondering why they left you. Gave you up like a diseased dog. It made you lose your self-worth. You fell apart from the inside. Never married. You reasoned that you could never love anyone because in the end, it would hurt too much to lose them. That's you, Agent Locke," said Jonas. "A woman without a past, and without a past, there is no present or future.

"And then there's Maddy." He grinned maliciously. "Poor little Maddy. A lovely child. Golden locks of hair. She loved the water. Nothing like a sparkling blue ocean, waves sucking at the toes of children playing with sand buckets on the beach. That's over now," he said flatly. "Instead of playing with dolls or giggling at the cute boy next door, she's buried under the sod with the worms. You let her die."

Emma's fists clamped. He was trying to knock her off

balance again. Make her shatter. She refused to break.

"You're not as smart as you think," said Emma.

"Jonas."

What?"

"Call me Jonas. I never did go for that formal bullshit."

Emma switched the subject. "How do you know about my sister Maddy?"

Jonas smirked. "I know lots of things. Call it a gift."

Holding steady, Emma smiled. "You know what I think Jonas? You're nothing but a second-rate killer. Not even worth the CIA hit list. Maybe you had a bad childhood. An abusive father. Is that it? Either way, there's nothing special about you. You're a shark feeding on innocent lives. Go ahead," she said smartly. "Tell me how great you are. How superior, because when it comes right down to it? You're just another leech feeding on society."

Jonas's eyes, soulless and dead, suddenly brightened. For an instant Emma swore something wolfish and inhuman stared back at her.

Not unlike her first visit, a shift in the temperature flattened the air. Heat climbed the walls by twenty degrees, baking the stagnant air. A Sulphur-like smell clung in her nostrils. Emma's heart beat faster. She grew woozy. Overhead lights, dusted with cobwebs, began to fade. The world shifted to another time. Another place.

And then suddenly she was there again.

10

Visions

Smash!

Glass exploded. Emma covered up. Her fingers clutched at rocks and dirt. A knife lay on the ground. Its blade glinted in moonlight. Picking it up, she got to her feet and stabbed the air.

Backing up, a ghostly white face stared brutally at her. Eyes cut into snake-like slits, he glared as if ready to bolt from the gates of Hell. Suddenly he charged and knocked the knife from Emma's hand. The blade clanged off rocks.

Lunging ahead, Emma reached out and frantically clawed at the assailant's face with her fingernails. Streaks of blood budded up on his cheeks.

Grabbing Emma by a tuft of hair, he flung her to the ground. Her bare feet, muddied with dirt, cut against jagged stones.

Emma's head hit something hard. Perhaps a rock. Her vision dimmed. Everything became clouded. She dragged herself over to her sister and covered her like a human shield. The assailant kicked her back with a heavy boot.

Sucking at the warm night air, he bent down and picked the

knife up.

"First your sister," he said. "Then you."

Leaving out an animalistic cry, he raised the weapon in the air.

11
Sleeping with the Devil

Emma's eyes blinked open. She gripped the tabletop and looked around. Visions of the intruder evaporated back into a dream. Stale air, damp with her own perspiration, burned away as the air cooled. She was back in the dank confines of cell number 6.

Jonas sat across the table. His oily eyes, ink stains, penetrated every hidden crawlspace of her entranced mind. He did it again. Got inside her mind. Festered there, a piranha feeding.

"What happened?" she asked.

"You drifted off. Maybe out chasing ghosts?" Jonas toyed. "You know what I think, Agent Locke? What happened long ago dictated your entire life. You couldn't help the people around you so you decided to join the CIA and save humanity. Ease the burden of guilt." He paused, his eyes bright as polished pennies. "Tell me more about that night. Even despots like me love a good sob story."

Emma held her chin high. "I don't need a confessional and you're no priest."

Jonas stared thoughtfully. "You've got me all wrong, Agent Locke. People don't get saved in my world. They die here."

Emma crunched her fists and remained steady. "You still didn't answer. Why did you request that I come here?" she asked again.

"Isn't it obvious?" His fingers tapped evenly on the tabletop. "You're a tin can filled with worms. I know what makes you squirm. That scares you, doesn't it? It's like sleeping in a blast furnace with the devil."

"You don't frighten me."

"Really?" Jonas mused. "Then why are your hands shaking?"

Emma glanced down. Steadied herself.

"Maybe you should run home," Jonas said. "Philadelphia, is it? The land of liberty. Instead of the CIA, maybe you can get job in some backwoods hot house, shaking that chicken shit little ass of yours. Better still. Find yourself a man. Shouldn't be hard. A woman like you must perform like a well-oiled machine under the sheets. The right man would make you moan. Scream for more. Convert you into a baby ranch. It's called the good life."

Emma pressed her lips tight together. Jonas continued kicking the tripwire, certain that she'd explode.

"You like games, don't you Jonas? I wonder if you ever looked at yourself or is that beneath the level of a narcissist? Remember those people you killed in the convenience store? They had mothers. Fathers. Did you think about that when you stuck the barrel of a shotgun under that cashier's chin and pulled the trigger? What about it? Did you ever love anyone enough to know the kind of damage you caused in the lives of those families? I doubt it." She shook her head. "Killing was a matter of consequence. They just happened to get in your way. Now I'm going to ask you one more time," she said. "Why did you request that I come here?"

Jonas crossed his arms. His eyes muddied like black water. "Why don't you ask poor little Maddy that question?" An air of confidence blanketed his voice. "Oh, that's right. She's rotting in some backwoods graveyard under dead leaves."

Emma stood motionless. Finally, she asked, "You're intrigued with my past." She paused. "Did you kill her Jonas? Did you kill Maddy? Is that what this is all about? Is that why you wanted me to come here?"

"And the fish nibbles the hook." Jonas smirked. "Enough questions for today."

"Answer!" Emma demanded.

"I said enough!" Angry veins ballooned in Jonas's neck.

The loud clang of a steel door opened. Lanster stood at the door.

"Agent Locke?"

Emma's unmoving eyes remained fixed on Jonas.

"Do you hear me?" Lanster snapped his fingers. "Time to go. Our friend is inside your head."

A guard walked in and touched Emma's arm but she pulled away.

"Tell me what I want to know," she demanded.

Jonas grinned hideously.

"Tell me!"

Emma stepped forward but the guards halted her. Staring intently, she turned and walked out the cell door.

12

Chatterbox

Just after dark, Emma stopped at the Sunset Lounge. The statue of a little green man holding napkins sat on the corner of the bar. Whatever secret surrounded Jonas Blackheart, it was as mysterious as the famed Area 51 itself.

"Need some company?" someone asked.

Emma turned to see Jason Diggs holding a drink.

Diggs had a golden glow on his face. Soft but rugged, all at the same time. Pulling out a chair, he sat down and sipped a bourbon on the rocks.

"When you signed up for the CIA my guess is you didn't think you'd be sitting in a bar on the Extraterrestrial Highway. Cheers." He raised his glass and took a swallow.

Emma tilted her head and smiled. "That's a given."

"We might as well talk about the elephant in the room." Diggs's voice relaxed. "I know about your past, Emma. Not a good scene," he said. "I was also told you're adopted, but that doesn't make what happened any less real."

Emma shifted uncomfortably. "I never knew my real parents. After that night, I tried to find them but couldn't. I even checked the CIA database but came up empty. It's a tough thing to live with. I don't know if they're dead or alive, if they loved me or just didn't want me."

Diggs reached out and touched Emma's hand. He ran his thumb over it. It felt soft. Warm. Made her tingle just a bit.

"What about the night. How much do you remember?" asked Diggs.

Emma lowered her eyes. "Sometimes I get flashes. For the most part it's a blur. I blacked out. At times it feels as if I'm on the verge of remembering, but it disappears like lightning on a stormy night."

Diggs released Emma's hand. "Don't worry. It'll come back some day. Then again," he added, "it's probably better if it doesn't."

Emma smiled and nodded. Uncertainty washed over her expression.

"Enough about me." She straightened up in her chair. "I've never been on the front lines. I don't know..."

"What you're doing here?" Diggs finished the sentence. Motioning to the bartender, he ordered another round. "Like I said. Jonas Blackheart requested you. If headquarters has more information, they're not sharing." Someone tossed a quarter in a vintage jukebox. A Jackson Browne tune played.

Diggs glanced out the musty window of the bar at the darkening and starry desert world. "Central Intelligence isn't always upfront about stuff," he continued. "In training camp, we referred to them as the undercover superman of America. I mean hell, whackos are everywhere. Rooting them out is about as easy as dancing on Jupiter. It pays to stay lowkey. Keeps the bad guys guessing."

A waitress brought another drink. Diggs took a swallow.

Emma played with her hair and caught herself staring at Diggs. He had a way about him. A twinkle in his eyes. Flirty but not obnoxious. Regardless of good looks, lines of stress played on his forehead. He tapped a finger on the side of his glass as if in deep thought.

"A few months ago," he said, "Intelligence picked up on a transmission from Syria. It wasn't your typical bullshit. You know, free political prisoners or turn Israel into a parking lot. This was different."

"How so?" asked Emma.

"We were holding a terror suspect in one of our tanks in Guantanamo. I know. Half the time they're closing up shop but we have our own private penthouse. Anyway, we bugged his room. He started jabbering to another prisoner about a plot unfolding in the states. We didn't buy in at first. Then chatter picked up on the internet. Targets got specific."

Emma visibly stiffened. "Another World Trade Center?"

"We wish it was that simple." Taking a last swallow of his drink, Diggs stood up and straightened his tie. He motioned Emma towards the door. "It's time you get up to speed."

13
The Dark Horse

Emma rode with Diggs up the dusty highway. They turned into the parking lot of the MARS building. Two rigid guards stood at the entrance. Flashing a badge, they opened the door. Diggs led Emma in.

Only one room existed in F section of the building. There were no windows or carpeting. The place had all the charm of an empty white box.

"Excuse the décor." Diggs knocked on the blank wall. "It's a safeguard against bugs."

Footsteps echoed in the hall. Lanster walked in and checked his Rolex. "What the hell? Can't it wait until daybreak?"

"It's time Emma gets in the loop." Diggs pulled a pack of cigarettes out and lit up. "Let me tell you something. Quitting smoking? It's a pain in the ass." He winked at Emma whose face remained fixed and serious. "Did you ever hear of something called the Black Death?"

Emma's eyes widened.

"For you people who aren't History Channel buffs, it killed more than 200 million people," said Diggs. "Rats and fleas were carriers. Symptoms began in the groin. Sometimes the armpits. People got sores the size of oranges that bled like stuck pigs.

"After that came smallpox," he continued. "It took out

about 500 million. The difference was it got passed through droplets of airborne saliva. Tumor-like lesions erupted on the skin. If you were unlucky enough to survive, let's just say you wouldn't be winning any Miss Universe pageants. Scars bordered on mutilations."

Emma sat stock-still. Her fingernails dug into the palms of her hands. The air conditioner hummed through the ventilation system, still a film of sweat gathered on her forehead. Diggs's momentary silence rolled in like a hurricane about to make landfall.

Dousing his cigarette in a Styrofoam cup, he said, "There's a new strain of virus on the horizon. The technical name is too damn long to pronounce. In layman's terms, it's called Dark Horse. The boys down at the Center of Disease Control in Atlanta aren't sure where it came from. The best guess is that it's a mutated offshoot of Ebola. The actual contagion rate is higher and the effects, much different."

An icy chill wormed its way down Emma's spine. "What happens?"

"It infects areas of the central nervous system. Creates a dead zone in the brain. Victims go into full blown dementia. They suffer violent illusions followed by complete memory loss. Problem solving, even the most basic functions, are gone. Some poor bastard could be sitting in front of a glass of water for days and thirst to death. The virus takes hold in a heartbeat. Someone could be driving down the expressway or flying a plane one minute, and the next?" Diggs leaned against the wall and shook his head. "Ironic, huh? We always thought things would go out on a nuclear blast. Who the hell ever thought the world's population would be decimated by Alzheimer's, all inside of a few weeks."

Emma fingered her throat. "Is there a cure?"

"CDC has the virus jarred up in an underground laboratory in Atlanta," Diggs said. "There's no antidote. Even if there were, making a vaccine for millions of people? You got better odds with the lottery."

Diggs stood quietly, his eyes two searchlights lost in the dark. He walked around the room and then turned to Emma.

"We have reason to believe a group of extremists got their hands on the stuff. They're threatening to pull the plug. Do you understand what I'm telling you?"

Emma stared. If Diggs's information proved accurate, the world stood a teardrop away from the next great epidemic. Mothers. Fathers. Children. There would be no division among victims or acquittal from the grave.

"Shouldn't we be alerting the public?" she asked.

Diggs shrugged. "Alert them to what? Nobody knows about this. If word got out there'd be International chaos."

A cold chill again wormed through Emma's extremities. Diggs was right. Panic would run rampant every time someone coughed.

"How do we stop it?" Emma finally asked.

Unfolding his arms, Diggs took a step forward. "That's where you come in."

14

How to Save the World and Influence People

Emma folded her hands and gently rocked on her heels. "This is insane."

Diggs nodded at Lanster. He pulled a small device out of his pocket. Pushing a button, a large map unfolded from the ceiling. New York was highlighted in red.

"According to our sources, the radicals have an operative in the Big Apple," said Diggs.

"Picture this," Lanster interjected. "A sleeper cell infects himself. The contagion rate is above ninety percent. The virus only takes 24 hours to be infectious but no symptoms occur for another five to seven days. Let's say this guy takes a walk in Central Park. Maybe does some window shopping at Macy's. Before the hour is up, thousands are infected. Over the next few days tourists move from state to state. Business execs board planes for other countries. Long before the first sneeze, the Dark Horse virus is roaming the continents. It isn't just an epidemic. It's the goddamn asteroid nobody saw coming."

Emma shuddered. "Do we have any leads?"

"We've located the head of the snake. He calls himself Butcher. Guess that fits," Diggs said. "The problem is, we need him alive. He's the only one who knows where the virus is. If he dies, his cronies have orders to execute the plan."

Emma listened in silence. Extinction rang in her ears. Town by town, city by city, the world would flicker out.

"What's our next move?" she asked.

Digg raised his chin and said, "Everything hinges on Jonas Blackheart."

"Blackheart?" Emma blinked. "Why?"

Diggs circled the room. For a man whose occupation relied on taking down entire enemy regimes, concern corroded every wrinkle in his expression.

"Jonas is a killer but he has special gifts," he said. "He can read minds. I know. It sounds like telekinetic bullshit, but it's true."

Emma flashed back to being in Jonas's cell. The room got hot just before she blacked out. Somehow, he got inside her head and spooned out the gory details of her tainted past. He brought them to life, almost as if she were there again.

"How did he get that way?" she asked.

Diggs looked at Lanster. The two men nodded at each other.

"That's enough for tonight," said Diggs. He pulled out another cigarette and lit up. The smoke swirled up towards the ceiling. "I hate these things. Quit for ten years. After my debriefing last week, I stopped in a mini-mart and bought a pack of Marlboro. If we're lucky, I'll have time to die from emphysema."

Emma shifted uncomfortably. "Diggs, this is crazy. I'm new. A rookie. You need a pro here."

"You still don't get it," he said. "Jonas Blackheart calls the shots. He wants you here. Why? Who the hell knows. But if we can capture Butcher, Jonas can get inside his mind. Read his mind. He'll be able to tell us where to find the virus." He reached down and touched Emma's hand and gently squeezed. "We can stop this from happening."

Emma paused. She looked in Diggs's eyes. "What do I have to do?"

"Whatever Blackheart wants. Just keep your wits," he warned. "This bastard is less than human. He'll play with your thoughts. Twist and shred them. Outside of the terrorists, he's the most dangerous person in the world."

15
The Circle is Small

Emma twisted on the sheets that night. It isn't every day someone tells you that the fate of the world is riding like a steel girder on your shoulders.

The following morning, hot sun rose over the desert floor. Wavy lines of heat lifted off the asphalt. Emma pulled into the parking lot of the MARS building. There were no signs of Diggs.

A GI toting a rifle again approached as she got out of the car.

"Morning." Emma held out her badge. "I need to get into cell number 6."

The GI tilted his head uncertainly. "Lanster isn't here. I'll have to radio him for clearance."

"Listen." She stared. "CIA takes precedence. I don't need Lanster's permission, understand?"

The GI backed up. The last thing he needed was Central Intelligence breathing down his neck. He'd be busted down to buck private. Maybe even sent to some shit island in the south pacific guarding an endangered species of frogs.

"Come." He motioned her in. "I'll need to inform Lanster when he gets here."

"Agreed." She nodded.

Leading Emma down the hall, he stopped at cell number six and unlocked the door.

———

Jonas stretched out on a dirty mattress. One leg dangled off the bed. The other was shackled to a metal pole. He didn't move when Emma entered the room. Eyes closed, his chest rose and fell in the dry stagnant air.

"I know you're here," he said, eyes closed. "I can smell the stink of your perfume." Finally opening his eyes, he leaned up on his elbows. "I'm surprised you came back. Maybe you're secretly yearning me." He grinned repulsively.

Emma's remained stiff. She lifted her chin and took a bold step forward, almost within reaching distance.

"We never finished our conversation," she said. "Why did you request me?"

Jonas swung his leg around and sat on the edge of the bed. "Because we're two of a kind, Agent Locke."

"I'll never be like you, Jonas. You're a killer."

"Long before this is over, I'm guessing we'll both be that," he said.

Emma tilted her head thoughtfully. "I blacked out when I was here. Saw things. Visions."

Jonas's eyes grew distant. "You were young back then. A budding teenager dreaming of prom dates and late-night fumbling's in drive-in movies. That night was a windstorm in dry leaves. It changed everything."

Emma's face hardened. She tried to remain emotionless. A poker player losing the battle of a good bluff.

"You keep reminding me of my past," she said. "I asked you this question before and you didn't answer. Are you the one who killed my sister?"

Jonas tapped his foot on the cement floor. "Let's just say bad things happen to good people, but enough of that. We're just getting to know each other. It's never good showing too much dirt during a first date. Let's move on."

"You're stalling," she said flatly.

Jonas stared. His eyes were razors. He was dissecting her; a specimen dipped in formaldehyde.

"You'd like to think you're in command, wouldn't you?" Jonas sneered. "Intelligence gave you steel balls but even the CIA can't harden the heart. That's your problem, Agent Locke. Clay guts. A caring soul. It's written all over you."

An underlying current of anger rose in Emma. Blackheart was playing with her again. She equated it to a child's prank, like sticking a garden snake down a young girl's blouse. He wanted her to squirm. Pull her strings. Watch her dance.

Jonas grinned with satisfaction and folded his hands. "Don't get quiet on me. Go ahead. Tell me what you're thinking. Dazzle me with that intellectual mind of yours."

Instead of stiff iron, Emma loosened her fists. She even smiled. "You're not so bad, Jonas. What was it, a lonely childhood? Is that what made you angry? I'm guessing you were one of those kids who'd rip the wings off a fly. Pokes it with stick. Make it suffer. Murdering those people in the convenience store made you feel strong. Like you were somebody." She lifted her head, elevating her presence. "You're not a monster or a king. You're a frightened little boy."

Jonas's weedy grin wilted. Peering in his eyes, Emma saw cold cement, cracked with age. Cheeks blushing red and lips pursed tightly together, he glared with contempt. Settling back on the bed, he put his hands behind his head and closed his eyes.

"You can go now, Agent Locke," he said.

Emma stood firm. "No comeback? You're a mystery Jonas. Even the CIA database is wiped clean. That's called a Code Red. Files aren't accessible for fear of the system being hacked and the truth coming out." She took another step closer. "Tell me what really happened to you?"

Jonas whirled around and unexpectedly grabbed Emma's wrist. She gasped and tried to pull free but he was too strong.

"You're a determined soul." Jonas stared, eyes black and hot as coals.

"Lanster!" Emma shouted. "Diggs!"

"Nobody can hear you." He gripped her wrist tighter. Pulled her closer. Sour breath flooded Emma's nostrils. "You really want to know what happened to me? Let's go down the rabbit hole, Agent Locke. That's what you want, isn't it? You want to know about the monster. The fiend. The killer in the dark alley. Lets' take a walk in the graveyard where you can smell the corpses rotting. The circle is small. Step inside."

A familiar heat swamped the unmoving air. Droplets of sweat shaped on Emma's temples. She grew dizzy again. Faint.

"Let go!" she shouted at Jonas. However, her voice sounded no louder than a whisper.

The overhead lights swirled. Faded. Once again, she drifted. The world fogged into an impenetrable mist. Jonas tightened the grip on her wrist.

"It's time to meet the man and the monster," he said, his voice shadowed in echoes.

Finally, Emma's eyes blinked shut. She felt herself falling into another time. Another place.

Part 2

JONAS BLACKHEART

16

Harbor Point, Years Earlier

Dressed in blue jeans and a button-down plaid shirt, the young man walked in the front door of Harbor Point. The building housed a number of businesses, chiefly medical constituents. A flaming redhead with freckles sat at the front desk and paged through a glamour magazine. She glanced over a pair of wire rimmed glasses.

"May I help you?" she asked.

The young man cleared his throat. "I'm here about a job." It occurred to him that he didn't even know what the hell the job was. Last week he saw the advertisement on the internet. He filled out an online application. Details were sketchy. The government put out feelers for a research program and needed recruits. "I got called for an interview. Someone named Jack Raison."

The receptionist checked her schedule pad and looked up again from behind her glasses. "Name please."

"Jonas," he said. "Jonas Blackheart."

The receptionist picked up the phone. "Yes, that's right. Blackheart." She put down the receiver. "Follow me."

———

Leading Jonas down the corridor, she stopped next to an office door and opened it. "Go right in Mr. Blackheart. He's waiting for you."

Jonas walked in and looked around. A large cherry desk sat in the center of the room. Except for a nameplate that said JACK RAISON in bold black letters and a Dilbert cartoon calendar, the top of the desk was empty. A burgundy leather swivel chair sat behind it. In the corner of the room, a wicker table clashed with the rest of the room's executive motif.

A stern looking man with a lantern jaw rummaged through a folder and looked up. His smile was stiff. Jonas swore the corners of his mouth would shatter like glass.

"Jonas Blackheart?" Jack Raison stood up and shook his hand. He snapped his fingers and pointed at a chair. "Make yourself comfortable."

Sweating bullets, Jonas lowered himself on the chair.

Raison dressed in a flawless black suit and red tie. The classic CEO hard ass.

Jonas fidgeted nervously. God knows he couldn't blow the interview. A senior at Pitt, tuition fees and rent drained his bank account. Extra cash would be a life saver.

Raison looked confident. Bold. He crossed his legs and draped an arm over a chair. "So, what can I do for you?"

Jonas stared blankly. "You called me for an interview." Fishing a resume out of his pocket, he pushed it across the desk. Raison pushed it back again.

"No need for that shit," he told him. "We're the big leagues. Nobody steps through that door unless we know what brand diapers they used as a kid. You're a psychology major at Pitt, right?"

"Yes sir."

Raison whistled. "Man, these days that's a goddamn thriving business. Whackos are everywhere." Picking up a breath mint from a tray, he popped it in his mouth.

Jonas smiled uncertainly. He sensed that Raison could turn on a dime. Submission was his best attribute if he wanted the job.

Raison rubbed his jaw as if sizing the candidate up. "You got any questions?"

Jonas shrugged. "What do I have to do?"

"Murder someone." Raison's expression turned serious as a heart attack. Suddenly he slapped the table. Jonas jumped. "Gotcha!" He laughed. Clearing his throat, he leaned forward. "We got rules here at Harbor Point. The first one is, never ask questions. The second is just as vital. What happens here stays here. Think of it like Vegas. We're government funded. Everything is top secret. We don't even release information to the President. Isn't that the shit?" He slapped the table again. "The pay is phenomenal. Beats cleaning toilets at one of the local diners."

"Yes sir." Jonas shook his head.

"All you need to do is sign a contract." Raison slid a paper across the table.

"Contract?"

"Just a formality. We don't like copouts." Jonas swore he heard a tone of warning behind those words. "We require our applicants to remain in the program for thirty days. Trust me. It'll pay all your tuition expenses and you'll still have beer money for Saturday nights. Just sign the waiver on the dotted line."

"Waiver?"

Raison barked, "Stop repeating me. You sound like a fucking parrot." Pulling a pen out of his shirt pocket, he tapped it on the tabletop. "We have one more opening in our curriculum. Either you're in or out. Remember. The job requires you to show up for thirty days. Quitters aren't welcome. We also have a no talk or die policy." He nudged Jonas on the shoulder playfully. "Seriously. Our business is classified. When you leave work, this place no longer exists. Understand?"

Jonas nodded.

Jack Raison handed him the pen.

Jonas stared at the paper. What was there to consider? He needed the job. George, his roommate, picked up most of the tab for rent and food over the last two months. If he didn't start paying, George would throw him out or end up moving to the dorms.

Leaning over, Jonas signed his name and looked at Raison.

"When do I start?"

17

The Red Zone

Traffic was bumper to bumper on the expressway. A turtle could have won a race.

"Come on!" Jonas thumped the horn. Slamming on the brakes he nearly plowed into a Sunday driver. Finally, the highway loosened up.

Motoring up the street, Jonas turned left on Forbes Avenue and pulled into the parking lot at Harbor Point. He checked the time on his cell. Damn! Late on the first day of work. Cutting the engine, he jumped out of the car and hurried up the walkway. Dungarees and a Van Halen tee-shirt probably wasn't standard attire but hey, the alarm didn't go off.

Jonas ran fingers through his mussed hair. He flung the big glass door open that led into the main lobby. Six people, college preppies by the looks of them, sat in the waiting room. Yawning tiredly and picking at their teeth, enthusiasm didn't run rampant.

"Name?" someone said loudly from across the room.

"What?" Jonas turned around.

"Your name please?" A stern looking Irish nurse dressed in a white medical coat stared at him.

"Jonas Blackheart."

The woman scribbled something in a book. "You make

number seven." She picked up a phone and hit a button. "Everyone accounted for Mr. Raison."

Gathering a bundle of papers, the nurse came from around the desk. "This way. No talking please."

———

Applicants were led down a long hall and herded into a room. The walls were colorless. Almost sterile. There were also no pictures. Aside from seven desks and a tray of donuts on a table, the room was empty. The nurse instructed the candidates to sit. A minute later, a familiar face appeared.

"Good morning,' said Jack Raison. He leaned against the doorframe sipping a steamy cup of coffee. The engraving on the cup read, *BOSSES are the SHIT*. Straightening his tie, he stepped into the room. His eyes clicked over the candidates. "So, this is the future of America, eh? Welcome to The Red Zone. Once you step in, there is no out door."

Jonas shifted his gaze from side to side. A guy with a bad haircut and earring sat next to him. On the other side a young girl, an auburn hottie, cracked a wad of bubblegum.

Raison placed a foot on a desk. He looked smug. Arrogant. Definitely in charge. After a frozen moment, he slapped a hand on his knee. "Time to get down to business. Class is in session."

Money or not, Raison's demeanor unnerved Jonas. He looked cold. Calculated. Piss him off and he'd rip your throat out for a dollar.

"We got ground rules here," said Raison. "Call it a cone of silence. Don't discuss what happens in here. That includes with each other. Easy, right?"

Heads bobbed and nodded. The young woman sitting next to Jonas cracked her gum again. He didn't know her name but recognized her from the campus.

Raison reached in his pocket and pulled out some papers. Holding them in the air, he said, "You all signed contracts. That means your ass is mine for the next thirty days. I'll give you one chance for a reprieve. If you're already turning chicken shit, the exit door is right there." He pointed. "Use it. You won't later."

The squirrelly guy with the bad haircut raised his hand. 'What if..."

Raison glared. "Rule number two. No questions."

The guy with the bad haircut slumped down in his chair.

Raison straightened his jacket. He walked around the room and eyed the candidates with careful intent.

"I've decided to candy-coat our arrangement," he said. "No reason. Guess I'm just a sweetheart feeling generous," he boasted. Everyone stared blankly. "There will be a two-thousand-dollar bonus after you complete the program. Who needs unions, right? We care about our dogs."

Applicants perked up at the sound of extra loot. Most college students, present company included, were busted. A couple of grand in cold cash would go miles and help fill the gas tank at the local Exxon.

"Keep this in mind." Raison's fist clamp tight around his coffee cup. "Negating on your contract is a big negative. There will be consequences."

Jonas's head tilted.

Consequences. It was an odd choice of words. Raison had

to be aware that he couldn't sue a group of college brats whose budget went no further than a Twinkie and a glass of milk for breakfast. In the end it wouldn't matter. The rent needed to be paid. Quitting didn't fit the itinerary.

Jack Raison picked up a pack of plastic cups sitting next to the coffee pot. "It's time to get started. This is called piss in a cup."

18

Hosing it Down

Jonas unzipped behind a curtain. A snobbish nurse with a pointy nose named Nurse Becket stared. Hands on hips, she sniffed miserably.

"Hose it down," she ordered.

Jonas tried but still couldn't go.

"You're making me nervous," he told Nurse Becket. "Do you have to stand there and watch?"

Never flinching, Nurse Becket tapped on a table and waited.

It took Jonas ten minutes but finally he managed. Surrendering the specimen to the nurse, he was handed a glass of green juice. It tasted like vinegar and smelled even worse. Afterwards he was led into a room on the opposite side of the hall. Seven recliners were lined up in the room. A large movie screen covered the back wall.

A man dressed in a white smock picked up a bathrobe and tossed it at Jonas. "Dressing room is over there." He pointed. "Take your shirt off and put this on."

Jonas emerged from the dressing room a minute later wearing the housecoat.

Another bullish man sporting a goatee and muscles the size of Manhattan stepped in the room. "You're number seven." He slapped the back of a recliner. "Get comfortable."

The man with the goatee attached nearly a dozen electrode pads to Jonas's arms and legs. Afterwards he pulled a heavy strap across his waist. It clicked upon locking.

Fear swam in Jonas's eyes. "What is this?"

"Relax. It's just a precaution," the orderly told him. "People get anxious. It's like being sealed in an MRI tube. After a while you'll wanna rip the place to confetti. That's not on the tour."

An applicant beside him yawned. Nurse Beckett poked him in the chest.

"You're not getting paid to sleep," she warned. "Do it again and there'll be consequences."

A booming noise suddenly blared from a pair of Marshal amplifiers near the back of the room. The movie screen lit up. It swirled with bright flashing strobe lights. At times the audio grew melodic and soft as a distant echo of lightly tapped piano keys. Other times it thundered off the walls. Candidates were required to watch each burst of brilliant color. Two hours later, the overhead lights flipped on.

"Wake up boys and girls," Jack Raison said, clapping his hands. He stood in the rear of the room studying them like rats in a lab. He whispered something in Nurse Beckets' ear. She jotted it down on a notepad.

Raison cracked his knuckles. "And like that you fattened your wallet." He grinned but the smile quickly wilted. "That's it for today. Just a reminder. What happens at Harbor Point is private. Don't talk about it, even amongst yourselves. See you bright and early."

———

Jonas walked into the parking lot. One of the applicants, the girl from Pitt wearing tight jeans and a crème colored blouse, approached him.

"Man, was that freaky or what?" She flipped her hair saucily over her shoulder.

Jonas fiddled with his car keys.

"Did you hear me?" she repeated.

Jonas looked up. "I don't think we're supposed to talk about it."

"I'm Annette Sanders," she forged ahead. "How about that music and video? Bizarro!" She rolled her eyes. "At least they could have sprung for some Led Zeppelin. And how about all that pissing in cups. Who pisses in a cup?" She hesitated and looked at Jonas. "You gonna stick it out for thirty days?"

Jonas shrugged. "We signed a contract."

Annette laughed and stuck a defiant jaw in the air. "What are they gonna do if we quit, run over us with a truck?" Turning her head defiantly, she jumped in her car and took off down the road.

19
Head Feeds

The following morning, applicants again gathered at Harbor Point. Annette Sanders, the girl who spoke to Jonas in the parking lot, studied her nails. The rest yawned tiredly.

Sleep misted up under Jonas's eyes. He trudged over to a coffee pot. The geeky applicant with the bad haircut walked up beside him. Grabbing the non-dairy creamer, he dumped it in a Styrofoam cup.

"Larry Hicks," he said, nodding at Jonas.

Jonas gave him the once over. Most of the crew looked mutinous as unpaid union workers. Not this guy. A smile the length of Rhode Island cemented his face. He even carried a plastic pen protector in the pocket of his button-down shirt. Jonas remembered kids like that back in high school. Fodder for bullies who roamed school halls.

"Jonas Blackheart," he answered.

Larry's eyes shifted around the room and whispered, "What do you think is going on here?"

Jonas had no idea nor did he have a chance to answer. Dapper in a fresh dark suit, Jack Raison walked in the room.

"I can see how enthusiastic everyone is." Raison grinned like an alligator. "Today's itinerary is simple." He held up a pack of plastic cups. "Piss in your cup, drink the green jungle juice and watch the film."

Nurse Becket took her post by the bathroom. She handed Jonas one of the cups.

"Hose it down," said the rude nurse.

Afterwards, Jonas was again handed a glass of green liquid that resembled pond scum. Another screening of the same video followed, only louder this time.

Electrodes tingling on his chest, Jonas pondered his part in the experiment. He once read that the CIA piloted a program called Operation Midnight Climax. It was designed to test narcotics by administering them to unsuspecting citizens. As he watched the psychedelic reds and blues crossing the video screen, he pondered the idea that Intelligence may have opened up shop again.

Leaning back on his recliner, he stared off into the lights.

———

The movie ended. Overhead lights flicked on. Jack Raison walked up the center aisle tapping a ballpoint pen on his hip.

"Another good day's work," he said. "I only have one issue. We got a fly in the ointment." He turned his head toward Jonas. "You spoke to another applicant last night after work." His eyes shifted to Annette Sanders and then back again. "Care to share?"

Annette's face dampened with irritation. "We just said hello," she said snottily. Judging by her expression, she might as well have said, "Screw you, asshole."

Raison stared suspiciously.

"It won't happen again," said Jonas.

Raison slanted his head. "Make sure it doesn't. Out there you're college preppies and fraternity pledges. In here? You're human research. Jackals," he said and turned to the others. "That goes for the rest of you. Don't break protocol. If you do, there'll be consequences."

20

One Week in the Hole

Jonas Blackheart stared dismally.

"Hose it down," said the ornery nurse as she handed him a plastic cup.

21

The Stumbling Red Rooster

The Stumbling Red Rooster had been a popular bar with the college brats for years. Lopsided neon beer signs hung in the front windows. Inside, sunken yellow lights were draped from wooden rafters of a high ceiling. Local bands like Becky and the Beasts and The Shellshocked Churchhills rocked the place every Saturday night.

Jonas Blackheart and George Patterson sat at a corner table in the bar. A song by the Stray Cats blared in the background.

"You look like crap." George slugged his beer. Setting an empty bottle of Coors on the table, he motioned to a curvy waitress with a Colgate smile to bring another round.

George and Jonas bunked in the dorm during their freshman year. They had been best friends ever since. The room décor included little more than grungy mattresses and a couch with coffee stains. George spent most of his off time in beat-up Nikes and studying tech magazines for computer science. Reruns of Beavis and Butthead took center stage on week nights. The guy had some quirks but he was a saint.

Prior to their senior year, they decided to split expenses. They found an apartment over on Liverpool. It wasn't the Hearst Mansion but college kids lived and thrived in the trenches. Lumpy beds. Clunky refrigerators. Old Farrah Fawcett posters hung on the walls. A dungeon or not, it beat the dorms. Furthermore, George wasn't a pain the ass like some of his other college buddies. He could tell the guy just about anything in the world without being called crazy.

"I haven't slept much." Jonas picked up his bottle and took a swallow.

"That's an understatement. Your head has been screwed on backwards since you started that job." George stopped to consider and leaned forward. "You know what you were doing last night?"

Jonas blinked.

"You were screaming in your sleep," said George. "It must have been a real scorcher of a nightmare. I sleep like a rock but heard you from the bedroom with the door closed."

Jonas chewed his lip. He didn't remember the dream. He did, however, wake up sweating at 1:11 with his heart pounding. Afterwards he paced the floors for an hour. Had to be those freaking movies at Harbor Point. They had all the charm of a bad acid trip.

"I've been under pressure," Jonas admitted.

George crossed his legs. "So, what happens at that new job you got?"

"I already told you." A hard edge shadowed Jonas's voice. "It's government crap. The guy in charge has all the charm of an crocodile in a Florida swamp. Says if we tell anyone what goes on there'll be consequences."

George tilted his head. "Consequences?"

Jonas shrugged. "Just forget it. I got other problems."

"What problems?"

"Mia. She's giving me the cold shoulder." He hesitated. "I think someone's cutting in. That's the last thing I need right now. Man, I'm crazy about her."

Jonas remembered the first time he saw Mia. It was at a fast food joint over on Hamilton. Tall and slender, she had killer eyes. Sure. She was flighty as a pigeon on a windy ocean. Her favorite cuisine included veggie burgers and peanut butter. She was a business major but her dreams never hinged on the corporate world. Mia wanted to open a shop by the ocean in Wildwood, New Jersey and sell flip-flops. Flip-flops! Crazy, right? Still whenever Jonas got close to her, he melted like candlewax.

George laughed. "You're delusional. Mia is true blue."

Jonas shrugged his shoulders. Maybe George was right. He hadn't been thinking straight. Still a suave med student from Pitt, Mr. Cool Toes, hadn't been his imagination. The guy hung around Cassandra's every night during Mia's shift at the diner. He was looking for more than a cup of coffee and sparkling conversation.

Taking a last swallow of beer, Jonas stood up. "Speaking of Mia, I told her I'd give her a lift home from the diner."

A waitress walked by and smiled. "Another beer?"

"No thanks."

"You sure?" she asked, a bit flirty.

Jonas slammed the empty bottle on the table. "I said no!"

The waitress moved on but craned her head around. She was used to rude customers. The look on her face said "total moron".

George slapped himself in the head. "Would you look at yourself? You're falling to pieces!"

Jonas stared listlessly at the table. Lately he felt confused.

Disoriented. Probably a lack of sleep. Insomnia began about the same time he started working at Harbor Point. The stitches in his frayed life had begun to loosen. He couldn't help but to wonder what might happen when the threads finally broke.

Tossing a tip on the table, Jonas abruptly walked out the door.

22

Ten days later and counting...

Ten days. Ten long freaking days of drinking green jungle juice, hosing it down and watching weird video flicks. The itinerary never changed at Harbor Point. Every day brought a fresh plastic cup to pee in. The only real modification came a few days back. Nurse Becket walked in the room with a needle and demanded a blood specimen.

Tension painted Jonas's forehead. Insomnia increased. He spent most nights walking from room to room, sometimes until sunrise. When he did sleep nightmares converged on him like red ants.

Jonas's dreams were equally bizarre. He was never the victim in his night terrors; he was the killer knocking off innocent bystanders. Clay birds in a duck shoot. Once he even dreamed that he chased Mia down a dark alley with a knife. Tackling her next to some garbage cans, he put the blade to her throat and... and...

Sweating profusely, he woke up.

Other times were equally as disturbing. He heard voices. When he turned to look, nobody was there. Not a good sign.

"You're walking the floors all night," Mia told him. "Maybe you should see a doctor."

Jonas stared in disdain. What the hell did she have to say

about it, acting all worried? These days she avoided him like the plague. They hadn't made love in over a week. Man, when they used to shake the bed, stars fell from the sky.

That changed when he began employment at Harbor Point. It was rare that Mia even offered a peck on the cheek. When he did try getting close, she had a headache or was tired. He knew the drill. Sure. She pretended to care. Acted all concerned. But looking at that blank stare of hers as they spoke? He just wanted to fucking kill her.

"Who's the guy hanging around the diner?" he blurted out.

Mia blinked uncertainly. "Shawn Ginders? Just a friend."

Closer than most, Jonas imagined.

"He's having trouble in physics. I'm tutoring him."

Jonas glared. Mia took a step back.

"Are you okay?" she asked.

Hands in pockets, Jonas looked at the floor. "I don't think you care anymore."

Mia hesitated. "It isn't that. It's ever since you got that job. You changed. Can't you see that? There's something different. Not in a good way."

Jonas couldn't help but to think about that shitty little elixir of green slop he was forced to drink every morning at Harbor Point. Who knew what was in it. Maybe steroids? Stuff like that messed up metabolisms. Made people aggressive. Dangerous. The other morning while riding a Sunday driver's bumper, he got out of his car at a red light and pounded on the windshield.

"Rev it up asshole!" he shouted and then got back in his car.

"Don't worry about me," he told Mia. "It'll be over at Harbor Point in a couple of weeks." He bent over to kiss her but she turned her head.

Jonas clenched his fists. Taking a deep breath, he loosened them again.

Mia walked to the window and stared into the street. "Maybe we just need some space," she said quietly.

And there it was. That goddamn "space" word.

First, she wouldn't return his phone calls. She'd go missing on selective nights. Then BAM! After the guilt wore off, she'd be gone, frolicking with Shawn Ginders, Mr. Cool Toes himself, a senior majoring in the medical field. She'd be sorry if that happened. She'd be sorrier than she ever imagined.

Jonas swallowed hard. "Is it someone else?"

"Don't be silly." She turned towards him, lying to his face.

But he wasn't being silly. He sensed deceit. Jonas couldn't pinpoint it, but it was almost as if he could read her thoughts.

"Jonas, you've got to believe me. We just need SPACE."

That "space" word cut through him like a samurai sword. Even worse, the evil little voice in the back of his head kept saying, *"Shut her up. Shut the bitch up for good."*

"Jonas, are you listening?" she repeated.

"What?" he answered, looking around as if someone else was in the room.

"You need time to get yourself together."

"Steak knives are in the kitchen drawer." A voice in his head said. *"You know what to do."*

"Are you okay?" Mia asked again. "Jonas?"

Shaking his head, he walked to the door.

"Get some sleep," she told him.

"I love you." Jonas softened up.

"Call me in a few days. We'll talk."

"Sure she will," the voice in his head invaded again. *"She's stalling. You'll call and get an answering machine. After that, enter Mr. Cool Toes. A guy like that? He knows how to satisfy a woman. She'll moan like hell all night under the sheets."*

"Jonas?" Mia asked again.

Turning, he walked out the door.

23

Annette Sanders had Enough

After two weeks of pissing in cups, drinking green monkey juice and watching psychedelic movies, tension grew.

Jonas walked in the bathroom and looked in the mirror. He picked up some weight. Not the fat farm kid, but brawny mass. Sleeplessness also left its mark. Dark circles shadowed his eyes.

Other applicants in the program didn't fare any better. They were lit matches under a leaky gas stove. Igniting a fire would only take a spark.

Annette Sanders looked particularly fidgety. She rubbed the palms of her hands together and shifted anxiously in her seat. A dark streak of mascara ran the length of her cheek. Greasy hair, once lustrous and flowing, ran down the middle of her forehead.

It was crazy. It was just freaking crazy.

When Jack Raison walked in the room that morning, tension was a balloon under a heat lamp. Minutes later, it finally popped.

"You guys look like swamp creatures." Raison laughed and set his coffee down.

Nurse Becket, Miss Charm herself, stepped forward with an arsenal of pee cups and clicked her fingers. "Everyone ready? Hose it down."

Annette Sanders visibly cringed. Slamming a fist on a desk, she stood up boldly.

Raison lifted an eyebrow. "Something wrong?"

Annette wiped a strand of oily hair away from her face. "Is something wrong!" she shouted in dismay. "I'm tired of pissing in cups. That's what's wrong!"

Raison glared. "It seems we have a ram among the sheep." He glanced at her chair. "Sit down."

Annette's hands shook. Dressed in a wrinkled red halter top, she looked like a matador facing off against a wild bull.

"It's always the same routine!" she shouted and pointed a shaky finger. "I want to know what's going on here."

Jack Raison remained composed. Thoughtful. He sat down on the corner of a table. Sipped his coffee. "I already explained, Miss Sanders. No questions. Now I'm gonna say it again. Set your little chicken ass down."

"Bullshit!" Annette shot back, fists balled up. She craned her head around and looked at her cohorts before settling in on Jonas. "Can't you see what they're doing? Are you all blind? We're mice in a maze. They're using us!" Covering her face with her hands, she began to sob.

The room grew stone silent. People studied the floor and desktops. Still, it wasn't fear that held the silence. Jonas could see it in everyone's eyes. They'd been beaten down to the carpet. Defending Annette Sanders would result in consequences. They just couldn't take another punch.

Smudged with dirt and clad in worn sandals, Annette stood there, a lone warrior on a sinking ship.

"I quit," she blurted out.

"You have a contract," Jack Raison differed and crossed his arms.

"Screw your contract!" she said. The cords of her neck stuck out, defined as telephone wire. "I'm calling the police. That's right," she said boldly. "I'm going to tell everyone what's going on here."

Jack Raison's eyes narrowed down to thin slits. "You don't wanna do that. I already explained. This is a covert program. Nobody talks about what goes on in here. If they do, there'll be consequences. You don't need that drama in your life."

Annette's eyes, pits of fire, stared coldly forward. She looked like a cornered animal. Unpredictable. Dangerous. Not quite human.

"I'm leaving," she announced, almost daring Raison to try and stop her.

Hands stuffed in pockets, Raison coolly held his ground. "You really want to go down that road? Then go ahead." He glanced at the door. "Get out."

Hesitation washed Annette's pale expression. It wasn't indecision but rather the darkening glare emanating from Raison's ominous presence.

Letting out a hideous scream, Annette toppled a table over. Plastic cups bounced across the floor. Turning once more to Jonas and the rest of the group, she shouted in a tearful voice, "You're dead. You're all dead and don't even know it!"

Annette hurried out the door.

24

Red Wine and Crackers
(21 days and counting)

"You okay man?" George Patterson sat on the couch in the apartment eating Fritos. Grabbing the remote, he flicked the channel to MTV.

Jonas mumbled as if talking to an invisible person.

"You listening?" asked George.

Jonas abruptly stopped. "I heard you. Now would you shut the hell up?"

A mounting rage in his roommates' eyes made George lower his head. In all the time that he knew him, Jonas never once slapped him down. That changed. It started three weeks ago, about the time he got the new job. Sometimes he'd wake up in the middle of the night to find the guy wandering the rooms. He was a freaking vampire.

George set the remote on the table. "You're not yourself," he risked saying. "Maybe you should rethink the job. Cajun Joe's is hiring. You could bus tables. I'll pick up the tab on the apartment until you get on your feet."

Jonas stopped pacing. "Nine days." He held up fingers and stared brutally. "Nine goddamn days and it's all over. Can you just shut up until them? Damn geek." He turned and began pacing again.

"Just trying to help," said George.

Jonas trembled, an inner rage ready to erupt. Why couldn't George clam up?

Wordlessly, Jonas marched over to the kitchen counter. He picked up a bottle of wine and smashed it against the wall. The bottle shattered and the wine trickled down the plaster, red as blood.

George's jaw dropped. Man, he saw some freaky stuff falling off the mountain but this was an avalanche. For the first time since bunking down with Jonas, he had no idea who the person was standing next to him.

It went beyond erratic behavior. Jonas hadn't showered in over a week. He smelled bad. Looked even worse. Frequently he talked to himself, almost as if someone else was in the room. The guy was skipping down a rabbit trail, heading for schizophrenia.

Jonas stared at the shattered wine bottle, almost as if trying to determine if he had been the one who broke it. He sat down on the couch and rubbed his hands tiredly over his face.

"Sorry man," he said. "Sometimes I think I'm going crazy. I know this is gonna sound nuts, but I hear voices. How screwed up is that? I must be crazy."

George stared. No argument there.

"You should get some help," he suggested.

"A shrink?" Jonas turned his head.

"I'm just saying. This entire thing started when you got that job."

"Would you shut up about the job!" Jonas's eyes rolled up, far enough to make the hairs bristle on George's neck.

George recalled reading about a serial killer a few years ago. His name was Eddie Kemper. He carried out a series of murders during the seventies. Even killed his grandparents. Later in life he blew a gasket and dismembered six female hitchhikers down around Santa Cruz. For an encore, he performed the coup de grace by taking out his own mother before turning himself into the police and riding the lightning. Looking at Jonas, he couldn't help wondering if Kemper was back for another round at the chopping block.

Standing up, George walked across the room. "I got classes tomorrow. Better get some sleep."

Jonas didn't answer. He gazed mindlessly at the blank wall.

That night George Patterson did something that he hadn't done since he moved into the apartment. He locked his door.

25
She's a little Runaway

Jonas woke up in the middle of the night. Unable to sleep, he went out and walked the empty streets.

Life had fallen into decay. He no longer attended classes at the college. It didn't matter. Hell, nothing mattered. Being labeled a dropout was low on the priority list these days.

Rounding a corner, Jonas turned up Basil Street. He stopped and turned when a shadow moved to the left of him.

A girl sat under a darkened beer sign at Banger's Pub. She had straggly blonde hair and wore cutoff blue-jeans. A torn red blouse draped her shoulder. Her eyes fixed as magnets, she rocked back and forth with hands cupped around her knees.

Jonas tilted his head in surprise. "Annette?'

Annette Sanders looked up. Instead of an attractive college coed at the university, he saw a homeless vagrant, delirious and confused. A fire burned in the ashes of her glazed expression and disoriented world. Crust lined her fingernails. She slapped furiously at her neck as if spiders nested on her clammy skin.

"What are you doing here?" Jonas asked.

Annette stared lifelessly into the darkness. A crumbled newspaper blew across her sandals, toes painted blue with chipped nail polish, but she took no notice.

"I haven't slept in days," she answered. "And the voices.

The goddamn voices never stop!" She raised her eyes. Hate swelled in them like a river. "They did this to us."

"Who did?" asked Jonas.

Annette glared. "Don't play stupid. You know who. Harbor Point." Dirty tears glistened her cheeks. She covered her face in her hands. "I'm falling apart. They wrecked me." She looked at Jonas again. "They killed all of us."

Jonas reached down and touched her arm. Annette pulled back as if bitten by a wasp.

"Don't touch me!" Her voice echoed in the silent street. She pointed a trembling finger. "You're working for them, aren't you?"

"I don't know what you're talking about."

"Don't lie!" Annette's words reverberated off the side of the building. "Harbor Point. They sent you to find me."

Jonas raised his hands and backed up. "Take it easy. I'm just trying to help."

Annette's fists clamped tight. "They used us Jonas. We're test monkeys. If it's the last thing I do, I'm gonna kill them. Don't try and stop me."

A bright candle of madness burned in Annette Sanders's tortured expression. Her eyes darted from side to side. Fierce as she was frightened, she had the look of a soldier, lost on some foreign field of death, ready to shoot her way out.

"You've got to listen Annette," Jonas said. "Whatever they did, it's happening to all of us. Sometimes I feel like I'm losing it. We need to figure things out. Get help."

"Help?" Annette laughed in surprise. "There is no help for us. We're already dead."

Standing up, she stuck a bony finger in Jonas's chest.

"Don't follow me. If you do, I'll kill you Jonas. I swear to God I'll kill you."

Turning, Annette Sanders marched briskly into the street. At that precise instant, the headlights from a black van rounded the corner.

Annette Sanders froze. The black van sped up. It struck her on the left side. She flew backwards, tried to hold her balance, but landed against the steel post of a parking meter.

Crawling on hands and knees, she shook her head and pulled herself off the blacktop. A film of blood circled her lips. Staggering like a drunk, she clung to porch railings and storefront windows as she made her way up the street.

The black van came to a screeching halt. Two men in dark suits got out. One ran behind Annette and grabbed her arms. The other held her legs.

Annette tried jerking free but the men were too strong.

"She's kicking like a mule," one of the men said. He elbowed Annette hard on the head, quieting her down.

"Hurry up," one of them said. "Cops will be here any minute."

———

Across the street, Jonas stepped off the curb. His heart beat like a hammer.

"Hey!" he shouted loudly. "Leave her alone!"

One of the thugs turned and stared brutally. Reaching underneath his jacket, he pulled out a pistol and took aim at Jonas.

"Put that thing away," his partner told him, holding firm to Annette's arms. "Don't you recognize him? He's a jackal."

The thug lowered his gun. Hate crossed his face, darker than a rogue wave. Turning, he slid the van door open.

Kicking furiously, they tossed Annette in and slammed the door shut.

"It won't go so easy next time, my friend," the thug pointed at Jonas and bent his finger as if pulling a trigger.

Jumping in the van, they revved the engine and disappeared down the road, almost as mysteriously as they arrived.

26

Tipping the Edge

Jonas hurried down dark alleys. He craned his head around to see if he had been followed. Reaching his apartment, he quickly went in and bolted the door.

"Think, damn-it," he said out loud and slapped himself in the head.

Did it really happen? It could have been a hallucination. Just the other morning he had a conversation with his Aunt Sadie. She passed away twelve years ago. Still there she sat, flowery dress and a golden smile, knitting on a park bench.

Then again, what if it wasn't a mirage.

Annette Sanders would be dead, that's what.

What was it that he heard one of the thugs say?

"You can't kill him. He's a jackal."

It hadn't been the first time that he heard someone use the expression. Jack Raison said it several times during their interment at Harbor Point.

The telephone suddenly rang. Jonas jumped as if stepping on a rattlesnake. He wearily picked it up.

"Hello?"

"Jonas?"

"Who is this?"

"I think you know," the caller said. "Take some advice. You didn't see anything tonight."

Jonas's thoughts raced back to Annette Sanders.

"I don't know what you're talking about," he lied.

"Keep it that way," the caller warned. "I'd hate to see you end up like your friend."

The line went dead. Jonas stared at the receiver.

———

The door of his roommates' bedroom opened. George stuck his head out and looked at the clock.

"Who was on the phone?" he asked.

"Nobody."

"Had to be someone."

"I said nobody!" Jonas shouted heatedly. Receiver still in his hand, he threw it on the floor.

"What's wrong with you?" George asked, his hand gripping the doorknob.

Jonas visibly cringed. An alien voice buzzed in his head.

"Your buddy just can't shut the fuck up, can he? You see that empty beer bottle on the table?" Jonas looked. *"You got any idea how easy it would be to smash it on the wall and then slit someone's throat?"*

Jonas whirled around, face damp with sweat. Nobody was there.

George stared. His expression bloomed with fear.

Kicking the coffee table, Jonas stormed into his bedroom and slammed the door shut.

27

Sticky Fingers

Rings of sleeplessness painted Jonas's pale expression. When he walked in the room at Harbor Point the following morning, the elephant stood boldly in the middle of the room. Annette Sanders's desk was empty.

Looking around, her abrupt departure wasn't the only thing amiss. A black crow hung on all the applicants' faces.

"We're dead already!" Annette's shadowy voice hung in his ears.

Larry Hicks, the geeky guy with the bad haircut, leaned over and nudged Jonas. "Stuff is going on here. Bad stuff," he whispered.

Startled, Jonas turned. "What?"

"I found out about some of the tests they're doing. I have proof."

Jonas set his Starbucks down on the desk. "What are you talking about?"

Footsteps echoed down the hall outside.

"We'll talk later," he whispered and sat down.

Jack Raison stepped in. He walked past Annette Sanders's empty chair as if she were never there. Nurse Becket tagged along behind him. She held a bundle of papers in her hands.

Whispering in Raison's ear, she glanced at Jonas.

Raison smiled; a wolf nosing in on a henhouse.

"Good news," he said. "We're going to forgo on the piss tests today but first we need to solve a mystery."

Everyone stared dumbly.

"Someone got sticky fingers." His eyes darkened. "They stole something from the facility last night. Security cameras are everywhere. We'll catch the guilty party. When we do, there'll be consequences. I'm a fair man." The applicants' heads tilted uncertainly. "I'm going to give the culprit a chance to come clean. Call it a reprieve from justice. Anyone want to confess?"

The room remained silent.

Raison tapped his fingers on a desktop. "I guess we'll do things the hard way." He took the stack of papers from Nurse Becket and glanced at them. "We're coming up on thirty days in the program. Long freaking haul, right? I'll be honest. I read the results of your tests. Some of you aren't cutting it. We'll be trimming fat in the next few days. If you're dismissed, you'll be notified by mail. Don't worry. You'll receive compensation on any remaining time you're contracted for." He walked towards the door. "Where our thief is concerned, he'll be hearing from us sooner than later."

28
The Times Tribute

Body of Missing Girl Found at Indian Lake

The body of a missing 21-year-old female was found dead at Indian Lake early this morning, face down in the water.

According to authorities, Annette Sanders of Meadville was pronounced dead at the scene after being spotted by some beachgoers. Other sources claim to have seen a woman answering to Sanders's description in downtown Pittsburgh the previous night.

"I saw her sitting on a curb. She looked out of it. Homeless. Almost high on drugs," one passerby noted.

An autopsy has been ordered to determine the cause of death. Foul play has not been ruled out.

"There were marks like she was in a struggle or maybe hit by a car," Ricky Troutman told police after stumbling across the body on a woodsy trail while out for a morning jog.

Anyone with information regarding Annette Sanders is encouraged to contact Meadville police immediately.

29

Oh Mia

Jonas stared at the headline in the newspaper. Annette Sanders was dead.

No. Not dead.

Erased.

Jack Raison had her killed. He'd likely be next on the extermination list. None of those consequences mattered for the moment. Other issues needed attending to.

Parked under a tree, Jonas crouched down in the driver's seat of his old beat-up Chevy. He stared at Mia's apartment on the opposite side of the road. A week ago, she told him she needed space. That space turned out to be larger than the Mexican border.

Earlier that day, he tried calling her.

"I'm sorry Jonas. It's over," Mia said flatly.

"But Mia…"

Click. The phone went dead.

The writing had been on the wall for weeks. Just the other night he saw her walk out of the library with Shawn Ginders. Mia swore she only helped him with some exams. Right. He knew guys like Ginders. Slick talkers. No brains. He moved in like a shark on the territory. It wouldn't take long before Ginders was checking out the hardware.

Jonas smashed his fist angrily on the dash.

Glancing in the rearview, he shuddered at the person staring back at him. Dark circles pitted against a ruddy complexion marred his face. Harbor Point had singlehandedly reinvented his life.

Jonas looked at Mia's apartment again. He pictured Ginders undoing her bra strap. Probably that one with the little red hearts from Victoria Secrets. Ginders had one of those big white slurpy smiles. Came from a family with lots of money. Nothing like buying the farm. Ginders would ravage her on the bedsheets, moaning with every thrust, all the while he sat crunched up in the front seat of a car drinking a warm beer from a tin can.

"I'll kill the bastard!" Jonas shouted.

An alien voice in his head answered the call, *"Then why don't you?"*

Jonas stiffened. He thought someone crept up to the window and whispered something. Turning around, nobody was there.

"You're losing it, old buddy," he said, giggling to himself.

Looking across the street, the lights were out in Mia's apartment. Probably lots of evidence to convict Mr. Cool Toes if he got inside. A disposable razor in the bathroom. Flowers on the kitchen table. Maybe even an empty pack of rubbers on the nightstand.

Jonas reached in his pocket. He fished out a key to Mia's front door. Thank God he had a duplicate made without her knowing it. He'd only need a few minutes to gather evidence and render a verdict.

"Followed by an execution," the voice echoed in his head again.

"Crazy, man." Jonas slapped at his ears.

Jonas scanned the streets. Sidewalks were deserted. He got out of the car and hurried alongside the hedges. Reaching Mia's door, his hand shook so bad he couldn't get the key in the lock. Steadying himself, the tumblers clicked and he pushed the door open.

———

Streaks of muddy light filtered in the windows from an outside streetlamp. The apartment was otherwise dark but he knew the layout. Hell, he should. He looked at the kitchen table, face glowing with nostalgia. Mia made love to him there one night beside a bag of Chinese takeout. Those days were long gone and buried in the dirt.

Whooshing the thought from his mind, Jonas surveyed the area. He had no doubt that Ginders had been cozying up to her. Still he needed proof. He'd need to risk turning on a light. Flipping a switch next to the dishwasher, an overhead light brightened the room.

The apartment was neat. Clean. That was Mia. Everything needed to be in its shitty little place.

Jonas turned on the hall light. He walked towards the bedroom. Outside of some pumps kicked in the corner by a closet, everything appeared in order. He opened a dresser drawer and rummaged through Mia's underwear. Didn't find much else but a box of tampons. Still no signs of Mr. Cool Toes. Not even a whisker in the bathroom from a shaving kit after a late night of rocking the bed springs.

If anything, it pissed Jonas off all the more. Never mind that he was breaking and entering. Mia went to great lengths to cover her tracks. God knows how long she had been hiding things.

Walking back in the living room, a light blinked on the answering machine. He reached down and flicked it on.

"Mia? It's Shawn Ginders." Jonas cringed. Speak of Satan, he rises from the ashes. "I'll see you at the library tonight. Just wanted to say thanks for all the help. Maybe I can buy you a drink sometime."

The message clicked off.

And oh my my. There it was. The gun smoked like a chimney in winter. Sure. Ginders didn't admit to screwing her brains out. He didn't have to. Circumstantial evidence was nine-tenth of the law. Mia lied. She'd pay though. Yes, indeed she would.

Jonas's cheeks turned wine red. Picking up the answering machine, he flung it across the room. It hit a mirror on the wall, smashing it to pieces. He continued by breaking all her dishes and crunching her television remote under his shoe. Hardly seemed like justice given his shattered heart.

Biting on his lip until it bled, he pulled a steak knife out of the drawer and marched back to the bedroom. He shredded the clothes in her closet. Grabbing a pair of lace panties draped over the arm of a chair, he flung them on the bed and stabbed them repeatedly with the knife. In a final thrust and warrior's scream, he rammed the blade of the knife through the undergarments, bone deep. Mattress springs popped at the force of the blow.

Jonas looked at a picture of Brad Pitt tacked on the wall. Giving it the thumbs up, he flopped down on the bed and ran fingers through his hair.

What had he just done?

Went crazy, that's what.

Did it really matter? Mia decimated his heart. She deserved it.

"She deserves worse," the voice in his head said again.

"Yes," he agreed out loud.

Jonas got up from the bed and walked down the hall to the front door. As if to add one more insult to the arsenal, he tore up a novel called Nesting with the Loons that she had been reading and tossed the pages in the air like confetti.

Flicking the lights off, he slipped back out the door. Neighbors undoubtedly heard the ruckus. Police wouldn't be far off.

Hurrying to his car, he turned the ignition but stopped cold. His lips flattened with anger. Down the road at Pulaski's Market. He could just make out two darkened silhouettes. Mia and Mr. Cool Toes himself, Shawn Ginders.

30

Mr. Cool Toes

Strolling up the avenue, Mia giggled like a bubbly teenager. Isn't that cute. Sweet sixteen again. She wore a black V-neck sleeveless shirt and a short chiffon dress.

Jonas knew the look. Guys talked about it in bars. Smoking hot and easy access. The problem was that the fire burned for Shawn Ginders. For all he knew, Mia just came home from a night under the stars and getting laid in the back of a pickup truck.

Talk about a kick in the ass. He just practically witnessed Annette Sanders getting murdered and she was out wetting her panties.

"What are you gonna do about it?" asked a voice.

Jonas didn't look around this time. He knew who it was. The boogeyman in his head.

Still, the question had merit. Mr. Cool Toes moved in on his territory. Circled her like a vulture. He crossed the line. Made a fool out of him. Picking up a box of Dunkin' Donuts as a peace offering and letting bygones be bygones didn't fit the itinerary.

One thing was certain. He needed to get the hell out of there. If police weren't already coming, they would be when Mia walked in her apartment. He trashed the place.

Jonas shifted his gaze back to the street. Mr. Cool Toes whispered something in Mia's ear in front of Pulaski's Market.

She laughed. Touched his arm. Ginders leaned coolly against a railing while she went in the store.

He looked more like a football player with a beer gut than a med student. Rock hard muscles. Probably steroids. Chances are he'd be laying pipe tonight. Mia's passionate moans would ring against bedroom walls.

———

Ginders gingerly kicked at a rock on the curb. His jaw dropped when he looked up. A car barreled straight towards him. Ginders' mind couldn't register fast enough for his legs to move.

Jonas waved a fist out the window like a cowboy twirling a rope at a rodeo. Ginders tried to get out of the way. Too late. The car ran over his foot and the bumper swiped his leg. He yelped and got thrown backward into a pile of garbage cans.

"Giddy up!" Jonas shouted out the window as he hit the gas.

Ginders floundered in the street. Hollering in anguish, he clutched at broken toes and a snapped ankle.

"Yeah!" Jonas shouted to himself as he sped away.

Flashing lights raced passed him. He turned up an alley. Skulking through backstreets with the headlights off, he came to a halt across the street from his apartment and quickly slipped in the door.

The lights were out. George was asleep.

"You did the right thing, cowboy," the voice in his head said. *"Mr. Cool Toes needed to be taught a lesson. You knocked him down. Broke a few bones. Next time we'll finish things."*

"Sure will," Jonas answered, surprised he spoke back to the invisible man.

Jonas yawned and trudged in the bedroom. He flopped down on the bed, fully clothed. For the first time in a month, he slept like a baby.

31

Alibis

The knock came on the door before sunrise. Wrinkled and unshaven, Jonas got out of bed.

"Who's there?"

"Jonas Blackheart?"

"Yes?"

"It's the police. We have a few questions."

Jonas cringed. He passed out on the bed last night. Convinced himself that the intrusion at Mia's house had been another hallucination. Judging by the men in blue, there were unforeseen circumstances. Maybe it was about something else.

"What is it officer?"

"Open the door," the cop ordered. "It's about Mia Wilson."

Bingo. The validation of a ghost. Last night really happened. Jonas dampened with perspiration. Brushing back his hair, he unlatched the door.

"Mia?" Jonas asked, putting on his best poker face. "What's wrong?"

"Her apartment got ransacked last night. Shawn Ginders, her boyfriend, also got rundown."

Jonas bristled. It wasn't the fear of wrecking Mia's place or clobbering Mr. Cool Toes with the car. The cop used the term "boyfriend" when he referred to Ginders.

"They're just friends," Jonas said with a stiff smile.

The cop tilted his head. "Excuse me?"

"Mia and Ginders. They're not together. She's just helping him with exams."

"Whatever," the cop said blankly. "What we do know is that you used to be her boyfriend." Jonas smiled bitterly. Yeah. The son-of-a-bitch was rubbing it in. "Where were you last night?"

"Are you accusing me?"

"Just answer the question."

"I was here all night."

The cop raised his brow. "Witnesses claim to have seen a car around in the neighborhood. It fits the description of yours. It was about the same time of the break-in at Mia Wilson's house and the assault on Ginders."

"Ginders?" Jonas repeated, almost as if he forgot the name.

"Mia's boyfriend," the cop repeated.

Jonas stared. No doubt about it. The cop was trying to piss him off. He didn't need the crap. Next time he'd just kill Ginders and get it over with.

"Ginders is a med student," said Jonas with a forced smile. "He's gonna make a fine doctor. Is there anything else officer?"

Jonas slid the door partially closed. The cop pushed it back open.

"I'll have to ask you to come downtown. We have a few more questions."

Confidence melted from Jonas's face and turned to uncertainty. He never even got a parking ticket. There's no way he'd survive a night in the slammer without killing a drunk.

A door opened on the other side the room. Tee-shirt hanging sloppily out of his pajama bottoms, George Patterson walked out and yawned. His eyes shifted to the police, to Jonas, and then back again.

"This is my roommate," said Jonas. "Tell him, George. I was here all night, right?"

George looked at Jonas who stared back with pleading eyes.

"He was here," George said slowly.

"You're sure?"

George nodded uncertainly.

The cop glared. He slapped a notebook closed in the palm of his hand. "I'll have more questions, Mr. Blackheart. Make yourself available."

Turning around, the officer motioned to his partner. The cops walked away and Jonas quickly bolted the door.

32

Confessions

"What's this all about?" George asked.

Jonas stood by the window. He watched the police cruiser disappear around a corner. Turning around he said, "Someone broke into Mia's apartment last night."

George looked up. "Don't you have the key?"

"Are you accusing me?"

"You haven't been acting normal. You're skipping classes. Pacing the floors all night. Flipping out for no reason. Sometimes when I look at you it's as if a stranger is staring back at me."

Jonas stiffened. His fists crunched. He took a deep breath. Stay cool, old buddy.

"Why should I have to explain things to you?"

"I'm just trying to help, Jonas. Hell, you haven't even taken a shower in forever."

"I'm warning you, George. You got nothing to say. Shut your trap!" Jonas shouted and immediately regretted his words.

"I got plenty to say." George took a stand. "I just lied to the cops. I have no clue where you were tonight."

Jonas sat down on the couch and lowered his head. "I'm sorry George. I don't know what's happening to me."

George paused and then leaned in. "I'm your best friend. If

you can't tell me, then you are screwed."

Jonas stood up and walked to the window. Finally, he turned around. "Listen to me. This is between us. If you tell anyone, there'll be consequences, understand?"

George nodded.

"The other night I couldn't sleep. I took a walk downtown. A girl named Annette Sanders got murdered. She was in the program at Harbor Point. Two men in a van ran her down. Afterwards they picked her up. Took her away and dumped her body by a lake. They know I saw them. I'm a witness, George. They'll be coming for me."

George's muscles tightened. "Did you go to the police?"

"It's not that simple. Harbor Point is run by a guy named Jack Raison. He's Al Capone reincarnated. If I blow the whistle on them, he'll order me killed for sure."

A loud moment of silence followed. Reaching over, George put a hand on his friend's shoulder.

"You can't go back there. You know that, right?' George said. "Maybe you should disappear for a while. Stay low on the radar. Get things together."

Jonas almost smiled. For the first time in a long time, he remembered stuff like cramming for tests all night or chilling down at the Alehouse on a Saturday night.

Still comradery would not last long. Jonas knew that. He faded in and out of reality daily. The man and the monster. If he shifted into werewolf mode, George would be in the line of fire.

"We'll find you help," George offered.

Jonas walked to the door.

"You're a real friend George. My best friend," he said, a tear gleaming in his eye. "I wanna keep it that way. I couldn't live with myself if anything happened to you. If anyone asks, you know nothing. Zero. Your life depends on it."

George stood up. "Where are you going?"

Looking back at his friend without answering, Jonas turned and walked out the door.

33

It takes a Thief

Jonas cruised the tires off his Chevy until finally hunkering down in a McDonald's parking lot. Once they found out he fled, it wouldn't take long until both the cops and Jack Raison hunted him down. He propped his head against the driver's window. Exhausted, he drifted off to sleep.

Flashes, red as blood, plagued his dreams. He was strangling someone. Was it a friend? Maybe even George or Mia? He didn't remember but woke up staring at his hands as if they belonged to someone else.

The cell phone rang, startling him. He didn't recognize the number. Could be a telemarketer or perhaps George calling from a different location.

Then again, it could THEM. He didn't show up at Harbor Point for work. Jack Raison would have the dogs out and sniffing.

Jonas picked up the cell.

"Hello?"

"Jonas Blackheart?"

"Who is this?"

"It's Larry Hicks. One of the applicants at Harbor Point. A jackal, just like you."

Jonas remembered him. A geeky guy. Horn-rimmed

glasses. Bad haircut. He told Jonas he had information and that they were all in danger.

"How did you get my number?" asked Jonas.

"I'm the thief," Larry said. "I stole a file folder from Harbor Point. Your number was in it. I also got other information. I don't wanna die." His voice cracked.

Jonas gripped the phone. "You're not gonna do something stupid, are you Larry?"

"Don't you get it? I stole their files. They'll be coming for me." He hesitated. "I need to give you something."

"Larry, listen...

"No, you listen! I'm over on Hamilton. Kline's Apartments. Know the place?"

"Yes, but..."

"Apartment 4C. Hurry. We don't have much time."

34

Apartment 4C

Hamilton was only a few blocks away. Jonas considered the idea that it could be a setup. Jack Raison and the goon squad might be waiting in ambush. Still, he couldn't ignore the desperate measures in Larry Hicks' voice.

It was getting dark. Jonas turned out the car's headlights to avoid being seen. He turned left on Hamilton and stopped across the street from Kline's Apartments. An old woman dumped trash in a barrel outside. Otherwise, nobody was around.

Jonas got out of the car. He hung close to the ground and ducked behind a fence. The front security door of the apartment complex had been jimmied open with an ashtray, no doubt compliments of Larry Hicks.

Slipping inside, he walked up the hall. Muffled voices of a couple arguing filtered into the hall. Something about meatloaf.

Jonas elected to take the stairs rather than the elevator to the fourth floor. Reaching the top, he peeked into the hall and then made his way towards apartment 4C. The door stood ajar. Pushing it open further, he stepped inside.

The lights were on. So was the television; a rerun of Jurassic Park. A half-eaten tuna sandwich and bottle of Doctor Pepper sat on the kitchen table. A sink dripped in a basin filled with dirty dishes.

"Larry?" Jonas said.

At first things remained silent but a bump in another room caught his attention. He walked slowly down a small corridor. Glancing in the bathroom, wet towels lay on the linoleum tiles next to the shower. A bottle of mint green mouthwash tipped over on the sink, dripped on the floor.

"Larry, you in here man?"

The lights were off in the bedroom. Curtains fluttered from a window in a warm breeze. Jonas stepped in. Someone stood on a dilapidated fire escape outside the window. Mussed hair blew in his eyes. A gun trembled in his hand.

"Hello?"

"Don't come any closer." Larry Hicks pointed the weapon.

Jonas froze and raised his hands. "Slow down. It's me. Jonas Blackheart. Put the gun down. Things are gonna be alright."

"You still don't get it, do you?"

"Get what?"

"We should have listened to Annette Sanders. Harbor Point is a cancer. We're dead as hell and don't even know it," he said.

Larry inched backward and his foot slipped off the fire escape. Arms flailing in the wind, he regained his balance and shakily pointed the weapon.

"It's happening to all of us, Jonas. Seeing things. Hearing voices. We're experiments. Lab rats under a scalpel. Harbor Point knew this would happen."

Jonas remained silent. Nothing made sense. He also couldn't dispute Larry's claim. Dementia. Schizophrenia. The demons swarmed. He remembered seeing Larry Hicks the first day at Harbor Point. Meek. Even nerdish, but now? Standing there looking down the wrong end of a barrel of a gun, things changed.

Larry straightened his glasses and shook his head. "Believe me. If you're not seeing ghosts, you will. The voices in my head. They won't stop!" He slammed the gun down on the iron railing of the fire escape. Rage turned to quiet remorse. "Do you know what I dreamed about last night? I was at home strangling my mother with an ironing cord, Jonas. Strangling her to death all the while the voices kept telling me to pull it tighter. You know what the worst part is? I was smiling. Do you know why?"

Jonas stood quietly.

"Because it wasn't me," Larry said. "It's that thing inside of me. The thing inside all of us. The monster." He looked closely at Jonas. "It's happening to you too, isn't it?"

Jonas glanced at the carpet. It started a while ago. Voices. Dark ones. Telling him to do things like wreck Mia's apartment or run down Ginders with the car. He looked back up at Larry.

"Killing yourself won't solve things. Put the gun down. We'll go to the police."

Larry raised his head and laughed. "It's too late for that. Jack Raison knows I took it."

"Took what?"

"I got suspicious about stuff. All those crazy films and tests? Something wasn't right. After one of the sessions, I stole the video they were showing us. I also swiped some files from

Raison's office." He pointed at a folder on the night table. "It's yours."

"Larry..."

"Take the goddamn thing!" Hot sparks lit in Larry's pulsing eyes. "Read it. Get it to the police. Don't waste time. They'll be coming. You'll be next."

Jonas picked up the folder and video. "Listen, man. Don't be crazy. We're stronger together. We can beat them."

"Beat them?" Amusement scratched Larry's sallow face. "Nobody beats them. They own the game board. We're puppets, Jonas. They pull the strings and we dance. They'll get rid of us the same way they got rid of Annette Sanders." Turning towards the street he looked off into the darkness. "You better leave now. No matter what happens, keep running."

"Larry..."

"Are you deaf?" Larry turned and pointed the gun again. "Go!"

Hesitating, Jonas turned and walked out. He hurried out of the building and crossed the street. Opening the car door, he abruptly stopped.

35

Midnight Flyer

A car with a blinking bubble sped around a corner. It came to an abrupt halt in front of Kline's Apartments. Two men in dark suits got out. Hanging tight to the exterior wall, they made their way to the entranceway and disappeared inside.

"Damn-it!" Jonas said aloud. He left the door wedged open.

It was dark but lights illuminated the parking lot and the drama that was about to unfold.

Larry crouched on the fire escape. Someone moved from behind the window curtains.

"Stay away!" Larry shouted, gun in hand.

Snap quick, a dark figure leaned out. He grabbed Larry's arm. The gun dropped. It clattered down the metal steps of the fire escape.

A second later, Larry Hicks went airborne. His limbs flapped like a bird learning to fly. He crashed against a railing on the second floor, hung there for a long second, and then plunged downward. He landed on the macadam in the parking lot with a hard thump, limbs twisted in impossible directions.

Dogs barked. A woman on the first floor ran out and screamed as if a UFO plummeted out of the sky. Fumbling with her cell phone, she dialed 911.

The two men in dark suits raced back out of the building. Before leaving, one of them reached down and checked Larry's pulse. After a moment of deliberation, he pulled out his gun, silencer intact, and shot Larry squarely in the head.

"Jackal down," he said to his partner. "Cops will be coming. Let's move."

On the opposite side of the road, Jonas ducked behind his car as the executioners spun their tires and disappeared down the road, headlights out.

36

Operation Jackal

Jonas drove, almost as if the devil himself chased him down the darkened highway. He pulled off on the side of a dusty road and tried to digest what happened. Annette Sanders got rundown by a speeding van. It didn't go that easy for Larry Hicks.

"Don't cross us," the voice of Jack Raison echoed in his head. "There'll be consequences."

Jonas glanced at the manila envelope that Larry Hicks stole from Harbor Point. He picked it up off the car seat and opened it. The front page of a document simply read, OPERATION JACKAL.

Reading further, the term Jackal was code for a mind control program dealing with telekinesis and psychic research. The government funded program initially began in the 50's. A scientist in the Swiss Alps named Nester Hyde discovered it. The report said the research enhanced supernatural abilities.

Jonas's eyes widened at the next paragraph.

Nester claimed he acquired DNA from a Russian defector after a UFO was rumored to have gone down in Urals, a mountain range that runs through western Russia. No concrete evidence was ever found but a decade later, Nester Hyde defected to the United States. He was taken to a newly established and secret military base in the Nevada desert known as Area 51.

The program was named Operation Jackal. Hyde continued his study until he died in the late 60's. The military was so impressed with his work that they funded the research under the jurisdiction of a government branch called The Agency.

Jonas's eyes shifted to the rearview. A winter chill frosted his spine. He fingered his face, almost as if examining alien flesh.

Turning his attention back to the report, he read further.

Select applicants affected by the JACKAL drug show significant signs of telekinetic aptitude after short-term use or within thirty days. Others remain unresponsive. In both cases, schizophrenia almost always develops. Subjects reportedly hear voices and suffer violent hallucinations. Symptoms increase with prolonged use and in withdrawal, applicants tend to become even more hostile. It's recommended that subjects be monitored closely for signs of mental illness or in some cases, termination.

Jonas felt as if a tractor trailer just clocked him after losing its brakes. If the report rang even half true, he wasn't just an absurd oddity of nature. He was the missing link.

A truck with bouncy headlights drove up the road, breaking his concentration. Jonas ducked down in the front seat. The truck continued on without incident.

Gripping the staring wheel, a runner of sweat ran down his cheek.

Think, man. Think.

Lay low for a while. Hide. Figure things out.

Jonas recalled a girl from his calculus class at the college. Megan. Yeah. That was her name. Megan Enders. Her family had a house up the road. The Enders lived in upstate New York but spent summer weekends barbecuing by the lake.

Megan threw a party last semester while her parents were in Manhattan. Booze parties for college kids were frowned on but security was sparse in the development. A guard patrolled the grounds about once every hour.

Jonas exited the car. The night air blew back his hair.

He began walking. It only took minutes to get to Megan Enders' summer house. No cars were around and the pool, empty. He didn't bother knocking on the door. Why screw with the small details. Glancing up and down the road, Jonas kicked the door until it buckled. A minute later it creaked open on broken hinges.

"That was easy," the voice in his head said.

"Sure was," Jonas answered the invisible man and slipped inside the cabin.

37

Megan Ender's Summer Swing Pad

The cabin had oak interior and a Swedish finish, complete with southern white pine floors. The kitchen opened into a large screened-in porch. It led to an outside grill that sat on a lavish mahogany deck.

It didn't take long to find what Jonas was looking for. He stuck the disk Larry Hicks gave him in the DVD player sitting on an entertainment center. Flicking on the TV, he picked up the remote and hit the play button.

At first the DVD showed nothing but the same garbage he seen at Harbor Point. Psychedelic colors. Star-like shapes of every dimension.

Fiddling with the remote, Jonas slowed the picture down. He saw nothing at first. Then there was an odd flash. Rewinding, he moved through the film, frame by frame.

"What the hell?" he said out loud.

The words were barely noticeable. Lightning bolts. There and gone. Only the subconscious mind had enough speed to grasp them. Words like *WE OWN YOU* and *KILL or BE KILLED*.

"Mind control," Jonas whispered aloud.

God knows how many people's lives Harbor Point destroyed by putting them through the wringer.

Jonas reached for the phone but stopped. Calling the police would draw him into the open. Jack Raison would kill him before he ever had a chance to talk.

Instead, he dialed his roommate's cell. Tell George. Maybe have him go to the authorities.

The phone rang and picked up.

"George?"

Hesitation and then, "Sorry. George is indisposed."

Cold sweat mopped Jonas's forehead. He recognized the voice.

"Raison?"

"Bingo!" Jack Raison said. "It's good to hear from you Jonas. We were getting worried."

"What are you doing there?"

"You broke the rules, Jonas. Remember what I told you back at Harbor Point? There'd be consequences if you bucked the system."

"What do you want from me?"

"I think we both know the answer," said Raison. "We had Larry Sander's phone tapped. He gave you something that belongs to me. He stole it from Harbor Point before he decided to take a leap off the 4th floor of his apartment."

"You killed him," said Jonas.

"All we want is our merchandise back.

"Will you leave me alone if I give it to you?"

"Sorry. You have a contract. Besides, we're way beyond a shitty subliminal movie and a couple of bogus files," said Raison. "You broke silence, Jonas. You told your roommate about our operation."

"George doesn't know anything."

Raison laughed out loud. "You think we're idiots? Phones aren't the only things wired. We've got every room in your apartment tapped. You told him all about us. You do know what that means, don't you? Don't make things worse. Turn yourself in. We'll shake hands. Maybe have a beer. Forget this ever happened."

"You don't need me," said Jonas. "You have other jackals."

"That's where you're wrong," Raison answered. "Annette Sanders and Larry Hicks are dead. The others were dismissed. Let's just say their piss tests weren't up to par. Most of them will develop schizophrenia. If they don't commit suicide, they'll be hauled away to some mental institution and never heard from again. That doesn't have to be the case with you. By now you're hearing voices. Maybe feeling a little crazy at times, right? I can help."

"Why would you help me?" Jonas asked.

"Because damn-it, out of everyone, all the college flunkies, homeless people and corner prostitutes, you're the only person to show real promise. You're the great white whale, Jonas. The seventh jackal."

"You're insane," Jonas said.

There was a loud noise and grunt in the background.

"Jonas!" someone shouted.

"George?" Jonas gripped the phone.

"Calling me insane isn't the best plan," said Raison. "It's like pissing in your boss's Cheerios. I don't like that word and wouldn't do it again. Now listen asshole." His voice grew deadly serious. "One way or another, you're coming back to Harbor

Point. As for your roommate George, I'm afraid it's a little more complicated. He knows too much. Consequences, remember? They suck."

"Leave him alone!"

Jonas heard George whimpering in the background. There was an abrupt silence followed by the loud blast of a gun.

"George!"

"Sorry. George isn't up to talking right now." Amusement raked Raison's voice. "A bullet hole in the skull will do that every time. Getting my message Jonas?" he asked. "You know, I got to hand it to you. Most of our applicants were crawling on all fours by this time. Not you though. You're tough as steel. I'm telling you, we're gonna make something out of you boy. One day you might even end up saving the world. I'm guessing you read all the files that Larry Hicks stole from Harbor Point. Schizophrenia will be settling in. Maybe it already has. You'll see things. Hear voices. Want to kill," he said. "There's a remedy for that. Just a little of that green jungle juice we've been giving you at Harbor Point will keep things in check."

"You'll pay, Raison," Jonas said in the receiver, his face shattered by thoughts of George's final moments on the planet. "I'll never come back."

"Give it time," Raison said smoothly. "Give it time."

38

I'll take Manhattan

Jonas Blackheart arrived at the 11th Street Greyhound bus terminal that afternoon. The foul stench of exhaust fumes lingered in the air mixed with cigar smoke of businessmen impatiently checking their watches. A woman with bags hurried by him and a ginger haired boy wearing baggy jeans and a Mets' sweatshirt stood on a corner holding tickets. People bustled all around. Still there were no signs of Jack Raison or his entourage on the street.

"You hear me son?" A man in a blue uniform stood behind a Plexiglas ticket window. "Where you headed?"

Jonas stared blankly. Good question. He had no idea. Even more, what would he do when he got there? It didn't matter. Annette Sanders's lethargic remains turned up by a lake. Larry Hicks took a plunge off a building. If Jack Raison found him, he'd be next in the toaster.

Looking up at the departure board, he said, "Manhattan."

Dirty as a vagrant living in a box, Jonas boarded a Greyhound. He eyed the driver with a goatee and sunglasses. Passengers were also scrutinized. No telling where or when one of the hostiles would turn up.

Opposite his seat, an annoying kid with ear buds tapped a foot on the floor. Behind him, a couple of foreigners, probably illegals, conversed in a different language. Some punk with an orange mullet puffed methodically on an e-cigarette.

Jonas leaned back and rubbed knuckles in his eyes. Sleep didn't come easy these days and concentration levels, bankrupt. He needed to stay focused. Danger crouched in the form of Jack Raison and his following of killers.

The kid with the ear buds in the next seat tapped his foot furiously on the floor to the beat of the music. Rock and Roll, no doubt. The noise pounded in Jonas's head like thunderclaps.

"Give that kid something electric, like a chair. Pull the switch," the rogue voice in his head chimed in.

Jonas never turned around. He knew the voice. The little bastard was like a knife, carving away at his sanity. When he got on the bus he even swore he saw a gunman opening fire on him. It'd be a miracle if he didn't get killed in the back of that Greyhound, right next to the portable toilet.

Jack Raison had been right. Psychosis sponged his head ever since he began treatment at Harbor Point. Frequently he suffered blackouts. Earlier in the day he walked six blocks to the bus terminal but remembered nothing until he found himself standing in front of the ticket booth.

Blackouts were only part of the problem. Sometimes he'd

shake uncontrollably. He craved the green slop that Jack Raison served up every morning of his tenure, the same way a heroin addict might lick his lips for a fix.

Jonas glanced over at the snotty kid with the ear buds, still tapping his foot.

Out of nowhere Jonas shouted, "Would you shut the fuck up!"

Pulling the kid's iPod out of his hand, he slammed it on the floor and stomped on it.

The kid's mouth was a gaping hole. Staring at the headrest in front of him, he remained silent the rest of the trip.

———

The bus chugged along. When it finally stopped, Jonas woke up scrunched in a cramped seat, somewhere in Manhattan.

"Hey asshole." The driver snapped his fingers at Jonas. "Last stop. Find somewhere else to sleep it off."

Wiping at his eyes, Jonas looked out the window. Tall buildings littered the landscape. People rushed here and there. It was official. He made it to the big time, home of the naked cowboy and bagel shops galore.

Jonas stepped off the bus into the bustle of the city. Hands in empty pockets, the obvious slapped him. He needed money and a place to sleep. Finding a job or knocking over a liquor store were the clear choices. The cash he got paid from Harbor Point wouldn't go far.

Once again, his cell phone rang. He recognized the number. Speak of the devil, Jack Raison appears. Against better judgement, he took the call.

"Hello Jack?" Jonas said sarcastically. "You're still the asshole, right?"

Raison laughed. "I'm glad you're keeping your sense of humor. You're going to need it before this is over."

"Give it up," said Jonas. "I'm not coming back."

"Oh, trust me," Raison differed. "You will. By now you've had some delusions. Blackouts, maybe. It gets worse. Much worse. Before the end, you'll crawl back to Harbor Point on hands and knees."

"Shut up."

"You sound edgy, Jonas. You got the jitters?"

"I said shut the hell up!"

"That's how it goes with you junkies," said Raison. "Cocaine addiction is a walk in the park. The green stuff you've been drinking? It's more like a bazooka blast. It'll knock you on your ass. Just ask Larry Hicks and Annette Sanders," he said. "So, tell me something hotshot. Are the voices getting louder? Maybe more insistent? It's a standard side effect. Psychosis is knocking on the door. You'll lose your mind before long, but you know something Jonas? I can change that. Tell me where you are. I'll pick you up. We'll let bygones be bygones."

Jonas cut the call and shoved the cell phone in his pocket.

A horn blared from an oncoming car. He jumped back on the curb. Some guy with a Fu Manchu mustache waved a fat fist out the window as he sped by.

Jonas began to walk. He passed shops that sold used clothes and shoes. Stinking of cheap liquor, a beggar sat on a step next to a vendor selling sausage sandwiches. The warm afternoon baked the city air. A steady flow of pedestrians streamed by him. Most of them looked busy and distracted. Still, he knew they were watching him. Spies were everywhere.

A ghost in the city, he continued walking. The hours passed.

39
Turning Points

Jonas found an apartment in a seedy neighborhood over in Washington Heights. It took most of his money he earned from Harbor Point. He looked around the dingy rooms. Painted paneling, a mouse hole in the baseboard and the smell of greasy eggs from Ed's Rodeo House filtered in from the back alley.

Staring out a musty window, Jonas pondered what he was even doing in Manhattan. At times he questioned if Harbor Point and Jack Raison were real or just an illusion. Seeing things happened a lot these days. When he first arrived in the city he sat down in a Chinese restaurant waiting for a takeout order of Chicken Chow Mein. A dark-haired woman walked in. He couldn't stop talking to her. The woman stared with bewildered eyes.

"What's wrong, Mia?" asked Jonas, cocksure that it was his ex-lover from back at Pitt. "Surprised to see me here?"

"I'm not Mia." The woman smiled nervously.

Perturbed, Jonas slammed a fist on the table. Chopsticks jumped off the table. "Do you think I'm a moron? I know exactly who you are." He pointed a stern finger in her face.

The manager, a big Italian galoot, walked over. "Is there a problem?"

Jonas brushed him away. "Can't a guy have dinner with his woman without some lowlife cutting in?"

Unamused, the manager stiffened. "The name is Frank," he said.

Outside of the cold steel from brass knuckles slamming him in the cheek, it was the last thing Jonas remembered until waking up next to a garbage dumpster in the alley.

———

Jonas landed a job washing dishes at Tickled Pickles, a joint over on the westside of town. The place served everything from high-priced hot dogs to London Broil. It wasn't just the money. He hoped working would keep his mind focused. Still the blackouts persisted. Once he woke up over a hot griddle with a spatula in his hand and no recollection of why he was there.

The boss, a squirrely guy with beard stubble and ketchup stains on his apron, approached him about his work habits.

"You're slacking Blackheart. I don't like slackers."

Jonas stared. A rising mist of rage stemmed from his crabby expression.

"You hear me?" asked the boss. "Pick up the pace."

For an instant Jonas had an impulse to throw his dish towel down and twist the little bastard's head off.

"Why don't you?" the rogue voice in his head whispered.

Jonas turned but already knew it was the invisible man. Still, it was a good question. A really good fucking question. He could hide behind the garbage bins in the alley. Wait for him. When he closed up for the night, bam! See how smug he'd be with his ears ripped off.

The boss got in Jonas's face again. "What are you, an alien? I'm talking to you."

Jonas smirked. If the stolen files from Harbor Point even remotely hinted the truth, alien might be the perfect portrait of his life. Untying his apron, he threw it on the floor and laughed so damn hard he nearly pissed himself.

Red faced, the boss pointed a bony finger. "You're fired, Blackheart."

Jonas grabbed his hand, twisting it to the breaking point.

A rising heat, as if someone opened one of the bake ovens, rushed through the kitchen. Dirty dishes went airborne. They smashed against walls and shattered. The boss looked in confusion, his mouth a gaping hole.

Contempt smearing his enflamed cheeks, Jonas let go of his hand and stormed out the door.

———

Jonas trudged back to his apartment. The episode at work still buzzed in his head.

What just happened in there? His mind clicked into the red zone. Dishes. Cups. Forks. Anything not nailed down took flight.

Shaking off the incident, Jonas stuck his hands in empty pockets. Yesterday he spent his last dollar at the 42nd street gun shop. The owner looked shady. A guy like that? Wave a little of the green stuff under his nose and he'd forego on the background checks and sell you a bazooka.

The gun store attendant smiled crookedly and handed Jonas a sawed-off shotgun.

"This is a nice piece," he said. "Sucker has an 18.5 barrel. Gives a good spread on a target. Home defense junkies are eating these up. It's just a matter of time before the NRA gets shut down by the democrats, the bastards."

After a moment of consideration, "I'll take it," said Jonas.

Standing in the living room of his apartment, stale crackers and peanut butter on the kitchen table, Jonas smiled as he felt the cold sleek barrel of the shotgun. He didn't know where or how his next dollar would arrive but understood there were always alternatives.

40

You give me Chills

Jonas woke up in the middle of the night with the radio on. The late-night DJ played a blues tune on FM. Nightmares again. He dreamed someone (or something) hunted him. He looked around the darkened room and honed in on the corner of an armchair. He swore a shadow crouched behind it.

Reaching alongside the bed, Jonas picked up the shotgun.

"Who's there!" he shouted. "Stand up or die!"

Jonas's finger cemented on the trigger of the gun. There would be no retreat. No surrender. If Jack Raison found him, they'd all go to hell in a fiery blaze. But nobody sprang up from behind the furniture. He was alone.

Sitting on the edge of the bed, he stared at the dull plaster walls, shotgun cradled in his arms. Twice he put the barrel in his mouth and jostled the trigger. Still he couldn't muster the guts to pull it. He threw the shotgun across the room, smashing a lamp, then folded his head in his hands.

"You're really screwed up," his invisible friend whispered. *"You don't even have the balls to kill yourself."*

"Shut up," answered Jonas.

"Listen to me."

"I said shut up!

Storming across the room, Jonas again picked up the shotgun and planted it firmly under the soft part of his chin.

"*Do it,*" the voice said.

"You think I won't?"

"*Do it.*"

"I'm telling you, I will!"

"*Pull the fucking trigger!*"

Jonas's finger twitched just as the cell phone rang.

———

Lowering the weapon, Jonas wearily picked up the cell.

"Jonas?"

Jonas stared. "Who is this?"

"Come on. I thought we were friends? It's Jack Raison. We know you're in Manhattan. What, you really think we can't track you down?" He laughed. "The next time you decide to purchase a shotgun, don't give your real name, dumbass."

"What do you want from me?" asked Jonas.

"It's more like what you need from us. You're seeing ghosts, right? Maybe talking to dead people. Goes with the territory," he said. "You ready to get the gorilla off your back?"

Jonas gripped the phone tighter. "I already told you. 'll never come back."

"You're wrong, amigo," Raison differed. "We didn't need to kill Annette Sanders or Larry Hicks. They would have done it themselves eventually. Is that what you bought the shotgun for? You gonna off yourself?"

"You ruined my life!" shouted Jonas.

"Calm down," Raison advised. "You don't wanna lose your perspective. Hell, we had one woman who snapped her daughter's neck like a pencil for playing video games. Ten minutes later? She didn't even remember doing it. That's the road you're on Jonas. A coldblooded killer."

Growling angrily, Jonas threw the phone against the wall.

Storming across the room, he stared out the window. Outside of a Chinese takeout restaurant, the alley below was vacant but not unoccupied. Jack Raison was out there somewhere. Waiting. Watching. Ready to pounce.

"You won't take me alive!" Jonas shouted into a warm sultry breeze that licked his face.

Whirling around, he kicked at a chair until he was out of breath, then staggered against a wall. He looked at the cobwebs dangling in dirty crevices of the ceiling tiles and thought about his disintegrating life. Crouching down in a corner of the room, he stayed there until dawn.

41

Outlaw Man

It was morning. A slow drip of instability leaked from Jonas Blackheart's disconnected mind. Whatever demon swooped in on his life, its iron claws refused to detach.

Jonas walked across the room and looked in a mirror. He was dirty. Gruff.

"Inhuman," he whispered.

None of those particulars mattered. His thoughts were dampened but lit with new horizons. It sounded crazy, even to him, but at times he swore he could read people's thoughts.

Just the other night he walked into Marigold's Liquor Store. The manager stood at the register, gold earring in his nose.

"I'm out of money." Jonas pulled at his pockets.

The cashier snorted. "What are you, a wise ass?"

His name was Marty. Jonas had no idea how he knew that. Marty wanted to lock up for the night. He didn't plan on going home to the wife and kids. A hot little Asian number down on 5th street had been waiting for him all night.

"She must be good," said Jonas.

Marty tilted his head. "What?"

"Alicia. That's her name, right?"

Marty turned three shades of pale. "I don't know what you're talking about pal."

Jonas leaned in. "Don't play stupid. Your whore over on 5th street. Better hurry. You'll be late."

Marty opened his mouth but closed it again. A stifling gust of heat blew through the liquor store, enough to make him stumble backward.

Jonas's steely eyes stared. "Give me all the money."

Marty blinked uncertainly. A dark mist shadowed his face. He reached for a gun under the counter but instead hit a button on the register. Pulling out a wad of cash, he handed it to Jonas.

Jonas grabbed Marty by the shirt. His gaze never faltered. "After I leave you won't remember any of this. As for your whore, that's our secret."

Marty nodded with dreamy eyes.

Picking up a bottle of Jack Daniels, Jonas strolled back out the door.

42

Mr. Peeps

Jonas returned to his apartment after leaving the liquor store. A steady buzz hummed in his head. Flies. It sounded like a swarm invading his skull.

The liquor store robbery was almost too easy. No doubt about it. His newfound telepathic skills were a gift, compliments of Harbor Point. Still, it wasn't as satisfying as the feel of sleek steel from a shotgun in his hands.

He had to laugh. A few weeks ago the biggest worry in the universe had been paying the rent and cramming for exams. Now he wrestled with demons and contemplated the joys of murder.

Jonas flopped down on the lumpy bed and punched the pillow. Shotgun cradled in his arms, he fell into a deep sleep.

———

"Blackheart, you in there?"

Jonas groggily wiped the sand from his eyes. Still holding his weapon, he pointed it at the door.

"Who is it?"

"Mr. Peeps, the landlord," he said angrily. "The rent is late. We don't take that shit around here. Pay up or pack up. You got until 5:00." Peeps pounded a hard fist on the door and then departed. His footsteps echoed down the hall.

Jonas giggled, almost hysterically.

Mr. Peeps? What kind of name was that? The owner was flat out rude. He should have emptied the shotgun on him. Chances are before the day ended, he just might.

"Screw him," Jonas said out loud, face scrunched as a wet sponge expanding with anger.

Looking down at the gun, he again fingered the shiny barrel. He thought about knocking over The Little Tiger, a convenience store over on 8th and Chew. That'd be worth at least a couple of hundred but it wouldn't go far. He needed a bolder plan.

A mouse ran across the carpet. It scurried into a hole in the woodwork. Jonas took no notice. He walked over to the window and stared across the alley, passed Max's Pizza Palace. He could just make out a billboard that read, First National and Trust.

"Yup." He twirled the shotgun like a cowboy. "Payday is just down the road."

The issue was decided. Jonas slapped his knee and headed for the door, shotgun in hand. Strutting down the sidewalk, he grew mortified when he stepped in a brown clump in the grass.

"Shit," he said, literally.

No doubt it arrived by way of an old bat who lived on the first floor with Muffy, a white yappy poodle. Scraping the mess off his shoe in the dirt, he vowed to come back when things were over and settle the score. Muffy would be a lawn ornament baking in the sun.

Dressed in torn blue-jeans and a blue hoodie, neighbors looked on in fright as Jonas walked by. He touted his newfound confidence that came in the form of an air of superiority and a loaded shotgun.

An elderly man watering the lawn dropped his garden hose when Jonas walked by. Shaking, he quickly disappeared in the house.

"Yep," he said out loud. "It's gonna be a good day in hell."

43

The Bank Job

It was a glorious morning. Sun shined. Birds sang in trees. That scenario was about to take a dramatic turn. Jonas appeared from the back of the building and approached the First National wearing beat up penny loafers and a green hoodie. Customers trickled in and out of the bank. Straightening his shirt and slapping a greasy strand of hair out of his eyes, he went inside.

A brunette with perky breasts worked one of the teller stations. Sasha Browne, according to her nameplate. She chewed the fat with another woman at the next station, Gwen Harter, a cougar with a low-cut blouse and curvy figure. Lackadaisical attitudes took a 180 degree turn when Jonas entered the room toting a weapon. Mouths dropped. A fat balding man with puffy cheeks screamed. Everyone raised their hands.

Jonas couldn't remove his eyes from Sasha Browne. She bore a striking resemblance to Mia, his college sweetheart. Hell, she even had a mole on her left cheek. Tilting his head curiously, he pointed the shotgun in Sasha's face.

"You following me?" he asked.

Sasha's expression shifted in extreme angles of fear.

"What," Jonas smirked, "not much to say Mia?"

"I..." she stuttered. "I'm not Mia. My name is Sasha. You have me confused with someone." Tears welled up in her eyes.

"Don't lie!" he shouted angrily, hands shaking on the gun.

Man, he hated that crap. She had him pegged for an idiot. Worse than an idiot; a moron. Eyeing her carefully, her suggestive blouse, cleavage for depraved customers, gave her the look of a street tramp.

A shadow moved from behind him. Jonas whirled around. Some geek in a white collared shirt and perspiration stains the size of pineapples inched forward.

"I'm in charge," he said, hands raised. "Please. We don't want anyone hurt. Take whatever you want."

Jonas shifted his gaze from side to side. A woman in an orange sundress huddled on the floor. Her pale expression was so bloodless she could have been mistaken for a corpse. Another guy in bluish kakis and a tank top tried inching his way towards the exit. Jonas gave him the stink eye, stopping him in his tracks.

"Stop stalling," the invisible man in his head prodded. *"Look at the cashier."* Jonas's eyes shifted to Sasha Browne. *"It's Mia. She wrecked your life. Spit in your face. Followed you. The cops can't be far. She'll laugh when they gun you down. Why take that crap from her? The shotgun is loaded. Put it to use."*

"Shut up!" Jonas shouted, seemingly to nobody.

The bank manager took a slow step forward.

Jonas instantly pointed the gun at Sasha Browne's head. "Stand down asshole! You want me to open this woman's skull?"

The manager stepped back again, legs shaky.

Jonas turned his attention to the bank teller. "How did you find me?"

Sasha shivered. "I don't understand. We've never met."

"Don't screw with me Mia!" A shine of madness glinted in his eyes. "I know it's you. There's even a damn mole on your cheek. Who has moles?"

Sasha pulled nervously at her hands. Black mascara ran down her cheek. "Please. I have two little girls." She glanced at a picture on the counter.

Jonas tilted his head.

Kids? Mia had no kids.

Jonas looked closer. Maybe this wasn't his ex-lover. Did it really matter? Glancing down at the shotgun in his hands, he blinked in confusion. What was he even doing here?

"Robbing the First National, that's what," the invisible man reminded.

"Hit the floor!" Jonas suddenly blurted out.

Customers and bank personnel fell to their knees.

Turning to Sasha he said, "Give me all the money. Now!"

Tears streaming, Sasha emptied the drawer with fumbling fingers. She handed him everything.

"You got a car, honey?"

Sasha glanced out the door at a teal colored Kia.

"Gimmie the keys."

Sasha fished the keys out of her purse. She shakily handed them to Jonas.

He again eyed the woman and whispered, "If I find out your Mia, I'll be back to finish things."

Raising the shotgun, he blew a hole in the ceiling. Tiles exploded and fell to the floor. Abruptly turning, Jonas walked out the door.

44

Harvey's Quick Mart

Sasha's Browne's Kia was parked outside the door of the bank. Jonas jumped in. Turning the ignition, he quickly pulled out and glanced in the rearview.

Nice. Real nice. The geeky bank manager must have tripped the alarm. Flashing lights from police cruisers barreled down the street. They were closing in fast. No doubt they'd have the roads blocked leaving town. It didn't matter. Nobody was getting out of this one alive.

Jonas hit the gas. He ran a traffic light and skidded around a corner.

Just up ahead, a quick mart sat on the side of the road. He pulled in and brought the car to a screeching halt. Whistling, he picked up the shotgun and got out. Jonas sniffed the air. It smelled clean. Fresh. Before the day ended, it would be painted red.

––––––

Jonas stepped through the door of Harvey's Quick Mart. Kicking over a newspaper rack, he raised the shotgun.

Mouths dropped. Over by the bread aisle, a woman with a

little boy holding a chocolate ice cream cone hit the floor. The guy behind the cash register, early twenties, instantly raised his hands.

Out in the parking lot, police cruisers converged on the place like maggots on rice. Lights flashed. Sirens wailed. Cops ducked behind cars and guardrails, guns bolted in their hands.

Jonas grinned. Raising the shotgun, he pulled the trigger and blew a hole through the rear wall.

"Ladies and gentlemen," he said. "I'm hoping to have your full attention today."

Turning to the guy behind the register, he glanced at his nametag.

"Hey man, you the manager? Roy, is it?"

Lips trembling, Roy nodded.

Jonas threw a five spot on the counter. "I'll take a pack of smokes. Make it menthol lights."

Roy said nothing. Shaking, he handed Jonas the cigarettes.

"Listen Roy." He leaned on the counter and lit up. "Some of your customers wanna be heroes. Nobody needs that. I mean, you're just trying to do a shitty minimum wage job, right? Cooperate and you'll keep these people alive."

Roy stared dumbly.

"Yes," he stuttered. "Yes sir."

Jonas looked around. He honed in on a guy over by the coffee island. He wore a construction hat and had tattoos lining his forearms. The superman type, no doubt. Given the opportunity he'd snap Jonas's neck like a chicken bone.

The construction worker stepped forward. Jonas turned and pointed his weapon.

"Excuse me, asshole?" Jonas asked. "You gonna listen or do I put a bullet in your head?"

The construction worker, aka Mr. Wonderful, stopped cold.

"See what I mean? They don't respect you," the invisible man rattled again. *"Even the cops think you're bluffing. Make a statement. Give them something to think about. Kill the store manager."*

"I can't just..."

"Bullshit," the invisible man cut him off. *"Do it. Let them know you mean business."*

"Shut up!" The shotgun quaked in his hands.

Frightened customers stood speechless as Jonas argued with blank walls.

A sudden rush of wooziness overcame him. He stumbled against a candy rack. Soon the conscious world would fade. He'd begin to drift. Tumble into a dream. The darkman in his head would take charge.

"What a pussy. You can't do anything right," the invisible man whispered. *"Enough talk. I'll handle things from here."*

With those words, Jonas fell into a blacked out.

———

The world around Jonas turned dark. He saw shadows. Heard echoes. Screams. It sounded distant as far off thunder. Other times it nearly cracked his eardrums.

Pop!

A loud noise. Maybe a gun discharging. Then more screams.

Swimming in a pool of darkness, Jonas looked around. He saw light in the distance. Cries of panic and terror got louder as he stumbled towards it.

As if emerging from dark tunnel, Jonas's eyes suddenly blinked open. He wrinkled his forehead, momentarily unaware of his surroundings. Red sprinkles dotted his shirt. The barrel of the shotgun smoked.

He gasped as his eyes shifted to the floor. Roy, the store manager, lay dead on the tiles. Thin runners of blood zigzagged through cracks in the linoleum from the gaping hole in his head.

45
Desperado

Jonas stared blankly at the shotgun. People in the store shrieked in terror. The woman with the little boy curled up on the floor covered her son's head.

Outside, frantic cops ducked behind buildings.

"You're surrounded," an officer yelled from the parking lot. "Give it up. There's no way out."

Jonas bit fiercely at his fingernails. He refused to look down at the dead body on the floor, almost as if ignoring it would make it go away. It didn't matter that he remembered nothing about wasting the guy. Nobody would believe him.

Grabbing a hysterical woman next to a soda cooler, he dragged her to the front door.

"We got a man dead in here." Jonas crouched behind the woman and shouted through an open crack in the door. "Don't think about firing. I'll put a slug in this woman's heart the size of grapefruit. Now back off!"

A brave cop stood up next to a police cruiser. "I didn't get your name."

"Hey asshole," he answered. "I didn't give it."

The cop stood there, frightened but composed. "We'll do

what we can to cooperate but I need some assurance. Release the hostages."

"You think I'm crazy?" asked Jonas, giggling at his own observation.

"I can't help unless you comply," the cop insisted.

After a moment of deliberation, Jonas pulled the woman back in the store. Sobbing, she curled up next to a magazine rack.

Jonas's eyes slid to another part of the room. He felt someone probing him. The construction worker, Mr. Wonderful again. He stared brutally.

The construction worker's real name was Melvin Crane. Other than the entity that took up residence in his disconcerted mind, Jonas had no idea how he knew that. He just did.

Melvin once beat a man senseless in a drunken stupor after the guy warned him about making lewd advances on his wife. He was also married. Had a little boy. Those were just distractions. He'd screw the bolts off a prostitute down on 6th street, then go home with a dozen red roses for his wife and toss a ball in the yard with his kid. He also did some jail time as a teenager. Something about assault with a knife.

"Hey Mr. Wonderful," said Jonas, gun pointed. "You with the pussy tattoos."

Mr. Wonderful glared. Jonas walked towards him and sniffed.

"Melvin," he said.

Mr. Wonderful blinked in surprise.

"That's your real name, isn't it?" Jonas shoved the shotgun under his chin. "You're quite the player. Guys like you know how to keep scum buried under a rock."

Mr. Wonderful looked in surprise. "I don't know what you're talking about," he lied.

"Really?" Jonas smirked. "What about Melanie Bates? A young girl. Maybe fifteen. You were out with the boys one night. A concert in Camden? Man, that was a real head banger night. You got a little drunk. Picked her up on a street corner. Raped her behind a parking garage. Afterwards, you beat her senseless. Left her in a dumpster in an alley, half dead."

"I don't know..."

"Bullshit," Jonas poked him in the chest with the gun barrel.

Outside in the parking lot, a cop took a step closer to the building. "You hear me in there? You got one minute to comply."

Grinning, Jonas stared at Mr. Wonderful. "You're a real cowboy. A desperado. I don't need that in my life right now." He nudged him forward. "Get the hell out of my store."

Fists clenched, Mr. Wonderful glared. It didn't look human or animal. Evil was the word. Turning, he started towards the door. Pushed it open and walked into the parking lot.

Jonas followed him to the exit door.

"Hey Mr. Wonderful?" he shouted. "You gonna thank me?"

Mr. Wonderful craned his head around. However, his cool demeanor was quickly rectified by a loud shotgun blast to the side of the head, discharged from Jonas's weapon. Mr. Wonderful dropped to the blacktop, dead on arrival.

———

Pandemonium broke loose. Police opened fire. Bullets

ricocheted off trashcans and an ATM machine. A chunk of hot metal plunked in Jonas's leg and then his arm. He also took one to the chest, buckling him over.

Falling to one knee, Jonas grinned and clamped down on the trigger of his gun, blowing holes in police cruisers. Finally, a cop hiding on a rooftop across the street, unloaded one to Jonas's upper torso.

Jonas dropped the shotgun. He fell down, flat on his back. Struggling for breath, the hot tar singed the hairs on his arms. He started to drift all the while smiling, as if the dark world encircling him finally reached its end.

Police officers gathered around him, weapons drawn.

"What the hell," a paramedic said. He checked Jonas's pulse. "He's still breathing. Not for long though. He'll never make it if we don't get moving."

"Promise?" Jonas heard one of the cops say smartly.

Forcing open his eyes, he looked up. A familiar face hung over him, black as a circling vulture in flight.

Jack Raison brushed back his hair in the warm wind. He bent down on his knees and say, "I told you, Jonas. One way or another, you're coming home to Harbor Point."

Jonas's hand felt around the hot blacktop, searching for his shotgun. Raison kicked it aside and out of reach.

"Don't worry," said Raison. We're gonna fix you, my friend. Your ass is gonna be mine for a long long time."

Standing back up, Raison snapped his fingers at one of the paramedics. "I need him alive. If he dies, there'll be consequences. Move!"

"Got a chopper waiting two clicks out," said the attendant.

"It's touch and go."

The paramedics loaded Jonas in an ambulance. Moments later, he closed his eyes and faded into darkness.

46

Back from the Rabbit Hole

Loud gunshots echoed in Agent Emma Locke's head. The impact of hot lead jolted her harder than a solid punch from a boxing glove. She opened her eyes. Confusion washed over her.

She was back in cell number 6. Jonas Blackheart held tight to her wrist. Foam dripped from his mouth in thick cords. The room temperature was sticky. Hot as Alabama heat in the dead of summer.

Staring through half-lidded eyes and breathing hard, Jonas unclamped his fingers. Emma sprang out of the chair.

The last thing she remembered was interrogating the prisoner. Then everything went dark.

No. Not dark. Misplaced. She moved to another time. Another place. The dry scent of burnt gun powder still clung in her nostrils. She looked over at Jonas. Somehow, he got inside her head. Gave her a glimpse of his unordinary past. He let her watch his world crumble and feel the bullets pierce his skin.

"What did you do to me?" she asked breathlessly, hands trembling.

Jonas exposed his stained molars in an ugly grin. "You wanted to know about my life, Agent Locke. Since we're practically sleeping together, I thought we'd dispense with the romantic bullshit."

Stifling herself, she stepped forward. "Is it true?" she asked.

"Is what true?"

"Jack Raison. The people at Harbor Point. Did they do this to you?"

Jonas closed his eyes and didn't answer.

"I want to know more," Emma said.

"I've told you more than enough. It's your turn, little Emma," Jonas countered. "Tell me about Maddy, your sister. What happened that night? The authorities searched for the killer. He disappeared."

Emma hesitated and swallowed hard. "I got a glimpse of him but can't remember. I blacked out."

"Post-Traumatic Stress Disorder," Jonas eyed her carefully. "Give someone something too terrible to remember and they shut off the terror. Build a wall where monsters can't reach them. Is that it? Your hiding from monsters?"

Emma's eyes narrowed. "I said I can't remember."

Jonas's lips curled. He leaned forward. "But I can," he said.

From behind her, the lock on the cell door clicked open. Lanster walked in and stood by the door.

"Agent Locke?"

Emma stared at Jonas. "I need more time," she told Lanster.

"Diggs is waiting for us," he answered.

Emma's eyes remained deadbolted to Jonas. "Was it you that night Jonas? Were you the man in the mask? Is that why you brought me here? You want to finish things. You want to kill me too?"

Jonas smirked sadistically but said nothing.

"Answer me!" Emma stepped forward, close enough to touch. Lanster stepped in. He grabbed her by the arm and pulled her back.

"We'll meet again soon, Agent Locke." Jonas folded his fingers. "Pleasant dreams."

Part 3

THE INSURGENT

47
The War Room

Lanster led Emma down steps that adjoined with a long hall. Only one room existed on the underground floor. A plaque on the door read, WAR ROOM. Seated at a transmitter, Diggs checked his wristwatch and looked up at Lanster.

"It's almost time," he said.

"Time for what?" asked Emma.

A dull buzz of static on the transmitter cleared.

"Agent Diggs?" someone said. "You there?"

Diggs's expression hardened. He picked up the receiver. "This is Diggs. Who am I speaking to?"

A pause and then, "You can call me Butcher."

Fractures of strain chiseled Diggs's face.

"Hey asshole, you still with me?" asked Butcher.

"You wanted to talk. Get on with it."

"That's what I like." Butcher laughed. "Cooperation. I'll tell you Diggs. My colleagues are pissed. The government is holding their boys in some shithole military base. Israel is another matter. They'd like the Jews to pack up the plantation.""

"Is that it?" Sarcasm tickled Diggs's throat.

"Not quite. I have my own agenda. My colleagues would like political injustices to stop, but me? I want twenty million dollars."

Diggs's eyes narrowed. "You're kidding, right?"

"Don't test me Diggs," he warned. "The government spends millions to save a rare monkey that's shitting in the woods in Africa. That's chump change. Consider the alternatives. You know the contagion rate of the Dark Horse virus. Imagine it. Millions of people with full blown dementia and Alzheimer's, all inside weeks. The freaking world is about to go nuclear."

Emma looked at Diggs. Patterns of stress lined his forehead.

"Aren't you forgetting something?" asked Diggs. "If the virus goes live, you're dead like everyone else."

Butcher laughed. "Don't insult me. I was a military man. Special Forces. American-made. Learned to prepare for disaster. Politicians and their mistresses won't be the only people barbecuing steaks in underground bunkers. I have a fallout shelter. Enough food and water to stay locked in until the virus burns itself out. Always figured I'd need it when some radical third world country got their paws on the bomb. Who knew I'd be the one pulling the pin."

Diggs's fingers crunched so tight around the receiver that his knuckles turned white.

"The United States government doesn't adhere to blackmail. Even if they did, it takes time to process a payment like that."

"Understood," said Butcher. "That's why I'm giving you 72 hours. Come on, Diggs. For a guy who takes down drug cartels and terrorist regimes, this is a cakewalk. I also know you're monitoring my position. Listen close," he warned. "If anything happens to me, my people are under orders to flip the switch. After that, the virus goes live and the planet goes red. 72 hour, Diggs. That's how long you have to save the world."

The radio went dead.

48

Magnificent 6

The War Room in the MARS building had no windows and the walls were plain white. Outside of a few chairs, the room stood empty except for a projector and radio.

Emma was seated next to the door when two search rats in military fatigues marched in. Crawling like human spiders, they examined everything from ceiling blocks to cracks in the linoleum floor.

"Raise your arms," one of them said to Emma. "Standard procedure."

Emma lifted up. The search rat patted her down.

"She's clean." He nodded at Diggs and left the room.

Within minutes, six commandos walked through the door. Four men and two women. Their uncompromising expressions sported stern jaws and military crewcuts. Each carried that "Don't fuck with me" attitude.

Diggs turned to Emma. "Meet our team. They'll be heading up the action once we get on the playing field. Intelligence refers to them as the M6. You might have heard of them around the water cooler."

Emma nodded.

During training, the M6, better known as the Magnificent

Six, were legendary. Prime directives were simple; seek and destroy, period. Outside of the military brass, nobody knew they existed. They were ghosts in the darkness. Gratification came in the form of fresh kills rather than public praise.

A few months prior a militia group planned to blow up the Golden Gate Bridge. The M6 moved in fast. Geared with night vision goggles, they crossed desert terrain and found the suspects in a basement in Loreto, just across the border. They killed 27 terrorists, most unarmed, and then went to lunch at Burger King.

Business as usual.

———

Diggs stuck his hands in his pockets. His grave eyes rolled over Emma and then the commandos.

"We just got word from headquarters," he said. "The green light is on."

One of the M6, a muscular female of Italian descent, raised a power fist. "When do we ride?"

Emma shifted uncomfortably in her seat and turned to Diggs. "What about the ransom money?"

Diggs said, "We have money if we need it. The feds don't want us to deliver it unless all else fails. Besides, Butcher wouldn't be satisfied. Sharks never stop feeding. He'd want more."

Picking a remote up off the table, he clicked a button. The lights dimmed. A projector in the rear of the room flicked on. The brutish face of a man shined boldly against the front wall of the room.

"This is the target," said Diggs. "He calls himself Butcher.

His real name is Edmund Rodrigo. We're not dealing with a foreigner. This bastard is American. He was born in Baltimore. Arrested on some minor charges but joined a militia group in his twenties. He's operating in the northeast. A small town called Jim Thorpe, Pennsylvania. We're not sure how many operatives are with him." Diggs hit a button and zoomed in on the suspect. "Burn this face in your memory. It's imperative we capture him."

A commando with a gold earring scratched his head. "You want him alive?"

Diggs nodded. "The success of the mission hinges on his arrest, not his execution.

"We'll be working in two teams," Diggs continued. "The first team's objective is to locate and capture Edmund Rodrigo, alias the Butcher. He'll be heavily armed and protected. The key is to dispose of his entourage without killing him."

Another commando raised a hand. "What about the other team?"

"They'll be guarding Emma Locke and her prisoner."

The commando stopped chewing his gum. "What prisoner?"

"Jonas Blackheart." Diggs shifted his gaze to Emma, who looked back in surprise. "We'll be flying at 19 hundred hours. In case you didn't notice, that's now. Check your maps. Get familiar with the terrain. We'll be arriving at ABE airport in Allentown Pennsylvania shortly after midnight. Two armored vehicles will transport us to the target."

Another commando raised a finger. "Guys like this never go down without a fight. Butcher might even commit suicide if he gets cornered."

Diggs didn't flinch. "I repeat. Keep the target breathing. If you see someone scoping him, even if it's your own teammate, take him out. It's that important."

A knock on the door diverted Diggs's attention. A soldier walked in and nodded.

"We're ready, sir."

49

The Load Out

Floodlights lit up the parking lot of the MARS building. Two military jeeps sat outside the door, engines running.

One of the M6, Hollister, shouted at the team, "Pick it up drag queens. This isn't a nursing home."

The commandos piled in one of jeeps and sped off down the desert road.

Emma and Diggs climbed into the second vehicle.

It took only minutes to arrive at the north gate of Area 51. A 747 was fueled up on the runway near a hangar. Two fighter jets sat adjacent the plane.

Two more jeeps pulled up on the tarmac. Lanster stepped out of one of them. Behind him and flanked by two soldiers, Jonas Blackheart exited the rear of the other vehicle. Legs shackled, he breathed deep and looked up at the brilliant desert sky.

"Move it along." A soldier nudged him towards the plane.

Jonas smiled as he walked by Emma. She warded off the compulsion to shiver.

Lanster stepped over to the jeep.

"Keep your heads out there," he said. "We'll be monitoring your progress from the MARS building. Good luck, if and when we meet again." Glancing at Emma, he nodded and walked away.

Hollister puffed on a cigar like a chimney. "Load'em up!" He twirled his fingers in the air. "Let's get the job done and be back in alien country in time for Happy Hour."

Diggs turned to Emma. "You ready?"

Swallowing hard, Emma got out of the jeep and walked up the ramp of the plane.

———

The commandos sat together in the rear of the aircraft. One of them cracked a wad of bubblegum. Another wore ear buds, tapping his fingers to a Bruce Springsteen tune. The rest looked out windows or nestled themselves against headrests.

Handcuffed and chained, Jonas Blackheart had been deposited near the center of the plane. He stared at Emma with a crooked grin as she walked down the center aisle.

"That one, Agent Locke." A soldier pointed at a seat next to Jonas.

Emma stiffened. "I have to sit there?"

"Not my call," the soldier said. "Blackheart is calling the shots. Guess he likes your company. No worries. He's secure."

Emma's emotions were tense as rubberbands, ready to snap at the slightest pressure. She quietly sat down.

"Beautiful night for flying," Jonas looked out the window. "Enjoy it. We'll likely be dead by this time tomorrow."

The rumble of engines fired up. The plane taxied down the runway. It steadily picked up velocity. The nose finally turned up and took off into the dazzling early evening sky.

50
Night Flight

The sun faded under the curvature of the world as the plane hit cruising altitude.

Diggs sat in the front of the aircraft studying a map and talking on a phone. No doubt Central Control.

Despite the rush of adrenaline and a madman chained at her side, Emma's eyes grew heavy. She drifted off to the steady hum of jet engines. What she dreamed about, she didn't remember. When she finally woke, she looked over to see Jonas's head tilted against the headrest. A disturbing grin drew over his lips. He began to hum an old lullaby.

"Hush little darling don't you cry..."

Emma stared forward, eyes fixed as magnets.

"... and if that horse and cart fall down, you'll still be the sweetest little baby in town..."

Jonas turned towards Emma. "Correct me if I'm wrong, but I believe that was one of Maddy's favorites."

Emma remained silent. The plane barely hit flight altitude and Blackheart had already started digging a moat in her head.

"You should go back to sleep," Jonas told her. "Dream good dreams. Enjoy what little is left of your life. Otherwise you'll end up like your partner." Jonas looked up at Diggs whose intense face studied the terrain on a chart. "Diggs is quite the character. CIA agents. They live for moments like this. Espionage and deception. It's the heat of battle. The excitement. It's what brought you all the way to the doorstep of Central Intelligence. You have me to thank for that, Agent Locke. I'm going to make you a legend."

Emma's guts churned. Ignoring Jonas for the entire flight would prove impossible. He'd continue to engage. Taunt her. She checked her wristwatch.

"We'll be arriving at ABE soon," she said coolly. "Get some rest."

"I'll sleep when I'm dead. That won't be long for either of us."

Jonas's eyes were murky as an alligator hid in sunken marshes. He liked playing games. Baiting the hook. Drawing her in and then gobbling her up.

"I blacked out in your cell." Emma switched gears. "I could see your past. Feel it happening. I could even feel you squeeze the trigger when you gunned those people down in the convenience store."

"You really think I killed them?" asked Jonas.

"I saw you do it," Emma said. "Somehow you made me," she paused, "be there."

Jonas twirled his thumbs. "That doesn't mean I killed them. Gacy. Manson. The truth is, killers are just little children playing in dark alleys that get lost. Leave them out there all alone and long enough, something snaps. It crawls out of a dark corners of their minds. Call it a demon. Suddenly everything changes. The killing begins. I should know."

Jonas glanced at the floor. It was the closest he had come to showing moral regret. Still, he tried to justify things. Play victim instead of the devil's advocate.

Staying cool, Emma asked, "Tell me how you read minds or make people see things in the past. It's almost like I was living it with you."

"People do it every day," he said. "Think of it as music. You're riding in a car. An old song comes on the radio. You haven't heard it for years. Still, you know every word. Every note. You smile because you think of those long ago sweet romantic teenage nights. Maybe fumbling in the backseat of a Buick at a lake under the stars. Suddenly, you're there again. That's me, Agent Locke," said Jonas. "I can make you be there again."

Emma forced a grin. "You're anything but music, Jonas."

"Dark music," he answered. "That's what I see when I look at you, Agent Locke. A sad song. Something too awful to hear because it brings back the memories of that terrible night long ago, doesn't it?"

Emma remained quiet. She loathed Jonas. Still, he was right. After that tragic night, psychologists tried to help her. Countless hours of interrogation and hypnotism proved useless. She glimpsed the face of the killer that night, still the torn flesh of her memory wouldn't mend. She couldn't remember.

"Stop the games," she said, her voice thick and confident. "You didn't request me on the assignment for no reason. We both know that."

Jonas's eyes deadbolted to Emma. "It's because you always wanted to be a hero. Dead leaves are blowing on your sister's grave, but just maybe if you can save someone else, you think you can make up for things. Change the river of blame inside. I'm giving you a reprieve, Agent Locke. A second chance. All you need to do is keep me breathing."

Emma turned away. "I'll do my job."

"Are you sure?" asked Jonas. "Do you really have it in you to keep a despot like me alive?"

"Why wouldn't I?" she asked.

Jonas grinned. "Because I'm the person responsible for your sister's death."

51

Killing the World

Tremors shot through Emma's heart. If Blackheart told the truth, she was seated next to the executioner that altered the fabric of her life forever. It made sense. She not only didn't meet Jonas before; she never heard of him. He chose her.

"You're lying," she said uncertainly.

"Am I?" Jonas smirked. "Police never found the killer. You couldn't identify him. All you remember was that he was a big man, like me. Think of the implications, Agent Locke. You've got a gun." He glanced at the Glock holstered on her hip. "My hands are shackled." He jiggled the chains. "Here's your chance. Pull the trigger. End that nagging ache in your heart and let justice be served. How easy would it be? Open a hole in my head the size of a grapefruit. Avenge the death of the lives you love while you watch my life drain away in a red puddle."

Emma involuntarily reached for the Glock.

"That's it," said Jonas. "Act on emotions. Who could blame you? Then again there's that little matter of saving humanity. Kill me and you kill the world. But does it really matter? Do it for poor little Maddy who's buried under the sod, worms crawling through empty sockets of bone." He moved his face in close. "I dare you."

Hand shaking, Emma removed her fingers from the Glock.

She took a deep breath. Needed to keep in control and stay focused. Maddy's fate happened a long time ago. If the mission failed, she'd have lots of company.

Jonas's black eyes bore down on her. He had her. The spider and the fly.

"I can see it." Jonas eyed her carefully. "The good little girl. That saint fighting against the evil of the world finally found her killer instinct. You want to pull that trigger."

A ding sounded on the intercom.

One of the commandos, Hollister, stood up. "We'll land in a few minutes people. Gear up. Paint your game faces."

Emma barely heard the order. She stared forward, crucified on a cross between rage and fear. Jonas's warm breath hissed in the backdrop against the rumble of engines.

"Nothing to say?" He smirked.

Finally, Emma turned. "When this is over, I'm going to kill you."

52

ABE Airport

ABE was closed to evening flights. Still the airstrip lights flicked on. The plane touched down with a thump at 11:17. Fighter jets turned off and disappeared, the roar of engines fading in the night.

Two armored vehicles disguised as vans sat on the runway. One sported a peace sign in rainbow colors.

"Kick some ass!" One of the M6 shook his weapon in the air as he exited the plane. He wore a headband with "De Oppresso Liber" scribbled on it in black marker, a Green Beret battle cry that in Latin meant "To Free the Oppressed".

Four of the commandos jumped in the lead van. The other two loaded Jonas Blackheart in the second vehicle and then got in the front seat.

Diggs approached Emma. "That's your ride. You'll be going with Blackheart." He bent down and touched her hand. Moving in close, for an instant Emma thought he might try to steal a kiss. Instead, he grazed her ear with his lips and whispered, "You'll be fine. Maybe we'll celebrate with some wine and dinner when the smoke clears."

Emma smiled. "Don't worry. I'll handle it," she said, although shadows of doubt clouded her words.

Climbing into the back of the van, Emma sat opposite Jonas. Electronic gadgetry and radar tracking equipment lit up the dashboard. None of it was of any consequence. Terrorists would wire themselves with a grenade and pull the pin rather than be taken alive. Forget waterboarding in Guantanamo or modern-day interrogation methods. Intelligence needed a mind reader to locate where the virus was concealed. They had only one weapon at their disposal.

"We meet again," Jonas said as Emma sat down.

"Unit two," a voice called over a radio. "This is Foxhound. We're ready to dance."

The commando behind the wheel picked up the receiver. "This is Bright Bulb. Green light is on. We're go."

Headlights on, both vehicles shifted into gear and pulled out on the highway.

53
A Homecoming

The vehicles used backroads. Taillights bounced off potholes. The commandos in the front seat studied the landscape as they drove. There was little or no talking about the mission. Fate would find them in its own time.

Emma couldn't remove her gaze from Jonas. Despite the urgency of the task, her mind continually drifted to the past.

What if Jonas really did enter her broken world years ago? He might have remembered her. Vowed to one day find her again and close the circle. Finish the job he started.

Jonas' s eyes opened, almost as if hearing her thoughts. Grinning slightly, he closed them again. Emma kept a firm grip on her Glock.

――――

Most of the road was dark and empty. They drove the thin white lines of the interstate until finally turning off on Route 443. Some miles down the highway, they crossed a bridge and turned on a mountainous road that traced alongside a river. Near the bottom of a hill, a sign read:

Welcome to Jim Thorpe

Gateway to the Poconos

A radio blipped in the front of the van. The driver put it on speaker. It was Diggs.

"We'll be approaching the target soon," he said. "Man. Talk about déjà vu. Remember this town Jonas? Must be a homecoming for you."

Jonas quietly gazed out the window. His unblinking eyes were dead pools of unmoving water.

Emma asked. "What happened here?"

"I explained most of it earlier," Diggs answered. "Jonas escaped from one of our sister companies. He made landfall in Jim Thorpe. Pisgah Mountain is to the right of you." Emma looked out the window at the blackened outline of trees in the backdrop. "Before being apprehended, Jonas made camp there. One of our boys shot him and he disappeared. When we finally found him, he was ducked out in an old mining shaft, barely breathing. We resuscitated him. How 'bout it Jonas?" Diggs said over the radio. "Keeping your ass alive is turning out to be career."

Jonas showed no signs of listening. It was the classic sign of a psychopath. He didn't care about life or death. Living amounted to pawns on a chessboard, ready to be taken and eradicated from the game.

"We're on radio silence from here on in until we reach the target point," said Diggs, changing the subject. "See you there."

54
Jim Thorpe, Pennsylvania

Entering town, the vehicle turned left. They passed the county courthouse and the Molly McGuire's pub. Victorian houses and small shops, mostly antique, lined the streets.

"Isn't that the shit." The commando driving pointed at a small music shop called Soundcheck Records. "I read about that place in a travel brochure. It's the last great independent record store in America. Some guy named Trooper runs the show. He's a freaking encyclopedia when it comes to vinyl."

Further up, they cruised by the Mauch Chunk Opera House, an old theater that played host to local talents and recording artists.

"This place gives me the creeps," the other commando in the passenger seat said. "During that stint in Afghanistan when we took down the mercenaries, I read this book. It was called CRUDE. Something about all the oil running out and the end of the world. You'd swear the story happened in this little town. Déjà vu, right?"

Traveling along, houses thinned and turned into little more than a deserted highway. Thick clusters of trees sprung up on both sides of the road.

The driver pointed at a thin reedy path in the distance.

"Right there," he said.

The van's headlights blinked out and turned down the woodsy trail, barely wide enough to drive through. Long branches scratched at the metal exterior like lean and bony arms. Two miles into the brush, both vans pulled over and cut the engines in a small clearing.

The commandos exited the vehicles, guns pivoting around the perimeter. Hollister made signals with his hands. The group formed a ring around the vans. Camouflaged in green, they blended like chameleons in tall reeds of grass.

"Silencers only," said Digg. "A campground is a few miles up the road. We don't need unwanted attention."

Walking over to Emma's vehicle, Diggs leaned in.

"What do you want me to do?" Emma asked.

"Stay here with Jonas. Two of the M6 got your back. If anyone comes, they'll be on it." He reached in his pocket and pulled out a key. "This unlocks Blackheart's restraints. If things go sour, get him out of here. Hide. We'll find you."

Anxiety swam in Emma's eyes. "What if..."

Diggs took her hand and squeezed it. "You'll be safe."

55

Closets

Diggs vanished in the darkness.

Emma shifted her gaze to Jonas. He stared at her as if in deep thought.

"We're finally alone," he said.

Ignoring the comment, Emma glanced out the window again. Things were silent. The calm preceding the storm. Still, she couldn't keep her mind on her duty. Thoughts of her tainted youth drifted in her head like lost and floating ghosts.

"On the plane," she said. "You told me you were responsible for what happened to my sister."

A smug look overshadowed Jonas's face. "That was a hot night. Humid as hell. The kind of heat that makes people crazy." He looked flatly at Emma. "Maddy suffered. She cried out. Called for you to save her. Remember her choking? Sucking at moist air. Those terrified eyes pleaded for clemency. But you don't remember all of that, do you Agent Locke?" he said smartly. "Sometimes it happens that way. We keep things buried in the closet. Sooner or later it opens and everything spills out. That's you, little Emma. You're trying to pick up bloodstains with your fingers."

Emma squeezed the handle of her Glock. Blackheart had her pegged. Led her to the edge of a cliff. Push a person too hard and eventually they'll fall off. He was daring her to cross the line and put a bullet in his head.

"You failed, Agent Locke." Self-satisfaction washed over him. "You failed to save you sister, and now you don't even have the balls to pull the trigger and take revenge."

For an instant the terrified face of Maddy invaded her mind. Trembling, not with fear but an inner rage, Emma raised the gun to Jonas's head.

56

Moles

Emma's finger froze on the trigger when sporadic gunfire cracked the night. Somewhere over the east ridge, bright flashes lit up the corners of darkness.

Jonas grinned in amusement. "The lions are restless. It's begun."

A commando scrambled out of a cluster of tall grass. His darkened silhouette moved rhythmically across the landscape.

"Incoming!" he shouted.

A bullet hit the metal exterior of the vehicle. Emma ducked. The van's door flung open. Diggs stood there. Breathing hard and face wet from damp heat, he looked energetic and fearful.

"Our cover is blown," he said. "The bastards were waiting for us. There must be a mole." Another bullet whizzed by, nearly clipping Diggs's ear. "Don't move. We're gonna try and take them down." He slammed the door shut.

Three more shots rang out. Emma looked from left to right. Spurts of fire ejected from weapons on all sides. The hostiles were moving closer.

Mad glitter sparkled in Jonas's eyes. "Exciting, isn't it? This is what you've been waiting for, Agent Locke. Time to save the world."

Blood pounded in Emma's ears. Fifty yards out, shadows moved across the landscape. A dark figure bolted out from behind a tree. A blade glinted in his had.

"Paisley!" a commando yelled. "Behind you! Get the hell out of there!"

Whirling around, Paisley grabbed the attacker's wrist. He twisted it until the bone snapped and then nailed him with a roundhouse right.

Paisley's partner emerged from behind a corner of the van. Clamping down on the trigger of his gun, he fired until the assailant nearly blew apart in pieces.

"Yeah man!" the commando shouted gloriously.

Glee turned to sudden surprise. Two more hostiles appeared from behind an embankment. One carried a machete. Hitting fast and hard, he landed a fatal blow in the spine of the commando, bone deep. Eyes wide and amazed, he slinked to the ground.

Paisley vaulted across the perimeter firing his weapon at will. Hitting the dirt, he pulled out his radio.

"Alpha, you reading me?" Paisley said frantically. "We got targets on the lawn. They're all over the goddamn place! Do you hear..."

Paisley stopped in mid-sentence. A stray bullet caught him in the throat. He made a wet, gurgling sound before dropping to his knees. He managed to get off another round, dropping one of the hostiles. Disoriented and fading fast, Paisley dragged himself on knees and elbows to the side of the van. Slumping against the back tire, he stared emptily up at the stars as he took his last breath.

Emma's arteries pumped with adrenaline. She scanned the perimeter. Bodies littered a reedy path beside the small clearing.

Fumbling with keys, Emma unlocked Jonas's restraints.

"We've got to get out of here," she urged, Glock pointed in his face.

Jonas looked at the gun. His stained expression was one of amusement. "No reason to be afraid, Agent Lock. There's bigger monsters than me in the forest tonight."

Trembling, Emma slid the van door open. Things quieted down, at least momentarily.

She pointed at a wall of trees that led into the woods. "We'll make for that ridge. Hide and wait for help."

Jonas lifted his chin in surprise. "Help?" He laughed. "There is no help for us out here. We're alone."

57

The Possum

Crouched under the stars, Emma pushed Jonas along a rocky trail. A soft rain began to fall. It spattered the leaves of trees. In the quiet of the forest, it sounded like steaks sizzling on a grill.

"Hurry." She rode the gun against Jonas's back.

Trudging through shrubs and thick grass, Emma abruptly stopped. Up ahead and near a small pond, a trickle of water played over rocks. Someone was on the ground. Stepping closer, her eyes widened.

"Diggs?" Dropping to her knees, Emma lifted his head off the dirt. Spatters of blood dabbed the corners of his lips.

Looking up at Emma, Diggs groaned. "I got blindsided. One of them caught me from behind. I fell down a hill and tore my leg on a branch." He fingered his knee and winced. "The bastard can't be far off." Diggs peered up at Jonas. "Keep him safe," he told Emma.

Emma looked around. "Where's the other commandos?"

"Ahead of me but they got caught in the ambush," he said. "They knew our every move. Someone tipped them off."

"Quiet." Emma put a hand over Diggs's mouth.

Footsteps tramped over leaves. Just across the perimeter a dark silhouette walked through the woods.

"We need to get out of here," she said, pulling at Diggs's arm.

Diggs struggled to his elbows and then back down again.

"Go," said Diggs, urgency painting his voice.

"I can't just leave you here to..."

"Go now!" he insisted. "I can take care of myself. We can't risk Blackheart getting killed."

———

Emma pushed Jonas across a shallow pond and up an embankment. They hunkered down behind a mound of rocks. The woods were thick. Directly behind them, the opening of a small cave hollowed the side of a ridge.

"Over there," she whispered, gun riding Jonas's backside. "Get inside. Hide. I'll try to take him out."

Jonas said nothing. His expression boasted amusement rather than fear. He faded back towards the cavern's opening. Emma squatted down, her eyes searching the night.

A twig snapped and a flashlight flicked on in the woods. The light shined around the trees. It came to rest on Diggs, who stayed stiff as a corpse.

The terrorist nudged Diggs with the barrel of his gun. Diggs didn't move. Looking into the forest, the terrorist pulled a cigarette out of his pocket and lit up. Exhaling a stream of smoke, he turned back to Diggs.

"You're playing possum, my friend," he announced. "I can hear you breathing." He stuck the gun barrel under Diggs's chin but his attention quickly diverted.

Storming out of the brush, Emma's finger clamped down on the trigger as she fired. Caught off-guard, the terrorist disappeared in a cluster of dense trees.

Emma's eyes darted from left to right. She moved slowly ahead. The forest grew still. Unmoving. Not even a summer breeze rustled the leaves.

Swift and furious, the terrorist bolted from behind a cluster of bushes and tackled Emma. Both of them toppled over and dropped their weapons. They rolled down a hill and landed in a basin of mud near the pond's outer edge. Twisting around, Emma raked fiercely at the aggressor's eyes. He released the grasp on her arm and drew his hands to his face.

Emma crawled up a small hill. Her chest rose and fell in fast rhythmic heartbeats. Her fingers squished in mud and dirt. Reaching the top, she pulled herself against the trunk of a rotted tree. The forest again grew still; dead stones frozen over in an icy winter chill. A shuffling noise near a rocky incline drew her attention.

"Jonas?" she whispered.

There was response.

Emma risked creeping out from behind the tree. A thorn bush scratched her neck. Wincing at the pain, she continued moving.

"Jonas?" she whispered again, a bit louder. "Where are you?"

The answer arrived with a hard blow to the back of the head. Emma's eyes closed and everything went dark.

58

Butcher

Emma' woke up in the dark. She sniffed at damp and musty air.

A kerosene lamp flickered in the corner of a room. The walls were dirt and stone; probably an underground cellar. Cobwebs draped the ceiling rafters. Dusty shutters covered a peeling window frame. It gave no hint of the outside world other than darkness. Candy wrappers and empty water bottles littered the floor.

Splinters from a rope stabbed her wrists. Tied to a wooden post, she struggled to get her hands free.

Hinges creaked when a door opened at the top of a rickety staircase. A man with a grayish scarf covering his face and a New York Mets baseball cap walked down the steps. Toting a rifle, he cautiously looked around the room.

"All clear," he yelled up the steps.

More footsteps drudged down the staircase. A man with black stubble littering his chin approached. Emma recognized him instantly.

"Pleased to meet you, Emma Locke. I took the liberty of checking you credentials." He held up Emma's badge. "I'm Butcher, but I'm guessing you already know that." He tapped the handle of a gun stuffed in a pair of faded blue-jeans. "Most of your friends are dead. If you don't wanna joint them, I'd cooperate."

Emma remained silent. She glanced at Butcher, sizing him up. He wasn't a big man. Then again, size didn't equate to danger. No doubt murder littered his rap sheet. Still, he wouldn't strap on a block of C4 and pull the pin. He wanted money. That meant he needed enough time on the planet to spent it.

"My operatives tell me you were with someone," he said. "He disappeared in the woods. Who is he?"

Emma breathed hard and fast. Still she said nothing.

"Not in a talkative mood?" Butcher bent down in front of her. "You'll tell me what I want to know. It just takes the right persuasion." His hand shot out and grabbed her by the throat. "Let's dispense with the formalities. Where is Jonas Blackheart?"

Cold sweat broke on Emma's forehead. A string of hair hung down the middle of her forehead, partially covering one eye. The question caught her off-guard. If Butcher knew about Jonas, the information had to be leaked. The CIA had a mole.

"I don't know what you're talking about," she said dryly, words trembling.

Butcher paused. He released her throat and slid a knife out from underneath his belt. Eyeing her from toes to hairpins he said, "You're a fine-looking woman. I'd hate to mess that up."

Emma's mind reeled. Words of her sworn obligation echoed in her head. Protect and serve, even at the threat of dying. Hands tied and staring into the face of a madman, that duty became harder to defend. Still, it didn't matter what methods of torment Butcher implemented to break her down. She couldn't comply. She left Jonas in the woods near a cave. By now he would have fled.

"I already told you," she said. "I don't know."

The henchman beside Butcher marched over. He slapped Emma hard across the face. His hand stung like a whip. A trickle of blood ran down her lip.

Butcher reached out and squeezed Emma's cheeks.

"I think you're lying, Agent Locke. But I'll give you some time to think about it. After that? The world gets bleaker."

Butcher stood up and doused the kerosene lantern. Motioning to his henchman, both men walked up the cellar steps and slammed the door shut, leaving Emma alone in the dark.

59
Pitfalls of National Security

Faint and silvery moonlight filtered through a small window in the corner of the cellar. Emma listened in silence. Rats skittered in the walls. Twice she swore the rodents dragged long hairless tails over the exposed parts of her ankles.

Shoes clunked on the floorboards upstairs. She heard muffled voices. She couldn't make out the words. Twisting her wrists again, she also couldn't break free. The knots were too tight.

How long had she been there? Minutes? An hour?

The cellar door opened again. A darkened figured walked down the steps. Instead of the kerosene lamp, he screwed a lightbulb into a socket attached to a wooden rafter.

Stark light blared in Emma's eyes. Focusing her vision, Butcher stood in front of her wearing a dirty tee-shirt and toting a semi-automatic.

A minute later, two more men were led down the steps.

Hollister, lead man for the M6 commando team, came first. Standing silent in the muddy light, his eyes surveyed the walls as if searching for a means of escape. Judging by the flower of blood on his shirt, he had taken one to the shoulder.

Butcher unexpectedly spun around and elbowed Hollister in the small of the back. Hollister groaned through drained cheeks and dropped to his knees.

———

Trudging behind Hollister, another familiar face emerged.

"Diggs?" Emma said.

Looking through bruised eyes, Diggs said, "Don't tell them anything."

Butcher grinned. He whirled around and kicked Diggs hard in the ribs. Diggs jetted backward and crashed into a support post before falling to the floor.

"You need some persuasion," Butcher said to Emma. He turned towards his henchman and nodded.

The henchman seized Diggs and dragged him over to a tub of filthy water in the corner of the cellar. Oily films of scum settled on the surface. Diggs's limbs twisted furiously as the henchman submerged his head. After a long minute, he pulled him back up. Diggs coughed and hacked.

"Jonas Blackheart," Butcher said to Emma. "Where is he?"

Emma's eyes crumbled in fear. She looked at Diggs who stared back wearily. Amazingly, the slightest hint of a smile played over his lips.

"I was pretty damn thirsty," he said smartly. "Don't tell him."

Butcher didn't seem amused. He circled the room, chin in hand. "You're funny, Diggs. Jerry Seinfeld, right?"

Butcher picked a dented soda can up off the floor. He poured the contents in the tub of water and then tossed the empty can aside.

"You're impressing the hell out of me Agent Locke, but you're going to talk," he said. "Do you know what was in that can?"

Emma stared blankly.

"Battery acid," he said. "It won't kill Diggs but it will eat his face off. You'll be next. Save yourself some pain and disfigurement. Tell me where Jonas Blackheart is."

Emma again looked over at Diggs. The expression of hard confidence written in his expression melted to an underlying softening of fear. For the first time in his career, Jason Diggs had hit a brick wall. There was no way out.

"Still playing the mute?" asked Butcher. He craned his head towards his partner. "Sink him."

"Wait!" Emma blurted out.

Butcher raised his hand. The henchman held Diggs's head an inch above water.

Emma stared at her adversaries. Agents were taught the mechanics of being interrogated in training drills. Still, the real world superseded any classroom exercise. Even Jason Diggs, an ocean of strength, had receded into a moat of uncertainty. Hair dripping and shirt shredded, his boyish good looks had all but disintegrated.

"You were saying?" Butcher asked.

"He was at the pond in the woods. He disappeared just before I got captured."

Butcher tilted his head and smiled. "I think you're lying. I heard about your mission. You're Blackheart's pet sheep. He wouldn't leave you cornered in a pack of wolves."

Grabbing the rifle from his partner, Butcher marched over

to Hollister and put the gun to his head.

Hollister knelt on the floor. You could see it in his face. There'd be no celebratory drink in a Nevada bar under an alien sky. His team was dead. He'd follow. Raising his head, he looked up at Emma with haunted eyes.

"Tell me what I want to know," Butcher said. "I'll kill him, then Diggs, then you. Where is Jonas Blackheart?" he ordered.

"I told you, I don't…"

"Answer the fucking question!"

"He disappeared and then…"

The sentence was interrupted by a loud shotgun blast to Hollister's forehead. Hollister hung on his knees for a blank second before falling to the floor with a sickening thud.

Stepping over the body, Butcher approached Emma and yanked her head up by a clump of hair.

"You've got three seconds. After that? Diggs takes an acid bath."

"Please. I don't know…"

"One," Butcher barked out, face beet red.

"I'm telling you…"

"Two!"

Emma's eyes locked on Diggs. Fear crawled over him like a worm in wet soil. For the first time in his life, the threat of dying became real. Even if he survived, he'd be hideously disfigured. Grim scenarios were the only passages into the dark future.

"Three!" Butcher sounded out. He nodded at his partner.

"The cave!" Emma blurted out. "I left him in a cave by the pond. He promised to wait there."

Butcher stared. "What else?"

"Nothing."

"Are you sure?"

"I'm telling the truth."

Butcher pressed the barrel of the gun against Emma's cheek. "That makes you expendable." His finger bent on the trigger.

Across the room, an unexpected voice rang out. "Wait."

Emma looked up. She stared in disbelief.

Diggs stood up. He spit on the floor and eyed Emma with distaste.

"Enough bullshit," Diggs said. Brushing off his knees, he turned to Butcher. "Don't kill her yet. We need her alive."

60

Sea Monsters

Cato brushed away branches and traipsed through the woods. The commandos were dead but didn't go down without a fight. Most of his mates were shot. Others had their necks snapped.

Myers, his partner, wiped a runner of sweat off his forehead.

"Butcher radioed in," he said. "Blackheart could be in a cave around the pond. He wants him alive."

"Quiet." Cato put a finger to his lips. He stared at a clump of bushes alongside the cavern. "Over there. To the left. Something moved."

Myers stepped forward. He looked into the blackened woods but saw nothing. Cato was seeing things again. Hell, that guy panicked faster than a rat on the Titanic.

"I don't see anything," said Myers.

Cato shined his flashlight around the cave's opening. "I'm telling you, someone's out there."

A quiet calm overtook the forest. Myers kept his rifle bolted in his arms.

Someone abruptly ran from behind a tree. Myers twisted left. He fired off a round. The bullet ricocheted off some rocks.

Leaping out of the bushes, someone speared Myers in the

stomach, bowling him over.

"Myers!" Cato shouted, gun zooming over the darkened perimeter.

A chilling silence followed a shrill cry and a sharp crack like bone breaking.

———

"Myers! Where are you?"

Spilling the beam of his flashlight around the edge of the pond, the light came to rest on his partner. Spread-eagled on the rocks, his head had been nearly twisted backwards.

Heart beating hard, Cato opened fire, discharging bullets everywhere. Peddling backwards, his foot slipped on wet moss but he held his balance. He halted near the rim of the pond at the bottom of a ravine. No way he could get across without moving downstream. The woods were thick as black sludge in that part of the forest. He'd be an open target for ambush.

He elected to wade through the water. It turned out to be shallow, rising just above his waist. Halfway across, he heard something from behind him. Turning around, he saw nothing.

"Freaking ghosts," he whispered under his breath.

Quickening his pace, Cato waded through the murky water. Once he reached the other side, he could hunker down behind some trees. Wait for the sonofabitch and mow him down without incident. He had no intentions of laying his life on the line. He'd take Blackheart out and bury him in the woods, then tell Butcher there was no trace of the guy.

Cato halted again. He heard something. This time he was

sure of it. Studying the darkness, his eyes shifted down to the surface of the pond, now nearly up to his chest. Moonlight reflected off the murky water. A stark gasp escaped him when he saw eyes staring back up at him, black and dead as a cold cadaver.

Lightning fast, a hand shot out of the water. It grabbed Cato by the throat. Cato struggled to loosen the grasp but it was tight as a wrench. Rising out of the pond, the assailant stared at him, eye to eye.

"Blackheart," Cato said blankly, mouth open.

Jonas grinned and hit him squarely in the jaw. Cato grunted and dropped his weapon. Tucking him firmly under his arm, Jonas pulled his prey across the pond to dry land and threw him down on a bank of rocks.

Gun floating somewhere at the bottom of the pond, Cato's defenseless eyes stared with expectancy. For an instant he swore Blackheart's face degenerated into torn flesh and grayish bone.

"What are you!" Cato shouted.

Jonas picked up a large rock and hoisted it over his head.

"Some people call me the Willies," he said. "You can call me Jonas."

61

Unexpected Company

Emma sat quiet in the sunken glow of the cellar. Of all the goddamn people in the world, Jason Diggs turned out to be the informant. He set them up. She remembered the touch his hand. That cool boyish demeanor and shy fresh-faced smile was an Oscar performance. De Niro would have been proud.

"How could you do this?" asked Emma.

Diggs offered a wily grin. "Don't be surprised. Espionage. It's hell on wheels."

Emma stared, a lock of hair falling in her face. "You're a traitor Diggs. Why?"

Diggs smirked. He wrapped his arms casually around one knee. "You really have to ask? Jonas Blackheart is a freak of nature. Hell, maybe even part alien if you believe intelligence reports. He can read minds. Think about it. If someone figured out how to harness that energy, no military secret in the world would be safe. How much would a foreign government pay to get their hands on something like that?

"I struck a deal with the extremists," he continued. "They get Blackheart and I'm given twenty million in cash, safe transport to an offshore island included."

Emma listened in quiet disbelief. Diggs stood up. Walking over, he bent down in front of her. She stared into his cold eyes.

Any splash of empathy he once showed had evaporated. He was a turncoat, not for principal or pain, but for money.

"The virus was a diversion," Diggs said. "The perfect lie to get Jonas Blackheart out of Area 51. Unfortunately for you, he insisted that you be involved. He's got some kind of weird connection with you. Freaking love. It makes people go crazy."

"You're lying," Emma said. "If Jonas reads minds, he would have saw what you were planning."

Diggs smiled. "Wrong again. Jonas is a mutant, but even mutants have limitations. He needs physical contact or at least in close proximity to get inside someone's mind. I kept my distance. You, on the other hand, were practically sleeping with him. He believed everything because you believed it."

A noise from upstairs diverted the conversation.

Diggs turned to Butcher and smiled. "Right on schedule. Romeo to the rescue. We have company."

62
Stranger in the Night

Butcher and his partner, Mendez, hurried up the cellar steps.

"Don't kill him," Butcher warned Mendez. "Take him out at the knees. We didn't go through all this to crate him up in a box."

The upstairs rooms were clear. Mendez looked out the window. He searched for a moving target. The silence struck him like a hammer. A dead calm sifted in the trees. The wildlife had been spooked.

Gun cemented in his hands, Mendez quietly walked to the door and opened it.

In a clearing by a makeshift campfire site, something rustled in the bushes.

"I'm not sure. Could be a squirrel," he said to Butcher.

The abrupt answer came in the form of one of the patrols, Cato or what was left of him, crashing through a glass door on the opposite side of the room. Butcher jumped back two steps. Mendez whirled around, eyes wide open.

Jonas Blackheart stood there. His teeth grinded together so fiercely you could hear the clench.

Mendez raised his gun but Jonas grabbed his arm. He hurled him across the room. Bouncing off a table, Mendez landed flat against a wall.

As if an oven turned on, extreme heat swamped the already sticky night air. Mendez imagined that he saw Jonas grow four inches, right before his eyes.

Jonas pulled a steak knife out of a holder on the kitchen counter. He flung it hard. The blade struck with such force that it pinned Mendez to the wall. Mendez hung there for a frozen instant and stared at the handle embedded in his chest. Slumping over, his head hung limply.

Turning his attention to Butcher, Jonas lunged ahead. Butcher overturned the kitchen table and bolted towards the cellar door. Diving forward, Jonas seized his ankle, tumbling him over at the top of the steps.

"Freeze, Jonas!" a voice rang out from the bottom of the staircase. "You hear me, boy? I'm talking to you."

Jonas peered down the steps where Diggs held a gun on Emma, probing her eye.

"I got your whore, understand?" Diggs said. "Maybe you don't care about your own life but I got a feeling you do about hers. I'll kill her. Right here. Right now. Now get your ass down here, nice and slow with your hands up. You got two seconds."

63
Little Edmund

Breathing hard, Butcher wearily got off the floor.

"He was down near the cave," said Butcher, keeping his distance. "He killed my men. One of them is in the kitchen after he used him as a human projectile."

Diggs kept the gun planted in Emma's eye. "One wrong move Jonas, I swear to God she's history." He motioned to Butcher. "Bring him down. Tie him next to her."

Butcher cautiously followed Jonas down the cellar steps. Nudging him over to a wooden post, he tied his hands around the support beam, opposite Emma.

"There you go. Nice and close to your tramp," he said.

A half-bent grin crossed Jonas's lips. "Maybe we're lovers," he said smartly.

"You're a comedian," said Butcher. "I'm told you were locked up in Area 51. Some kind of freak that can read people's minds. I don't believe in that telekinetic bullshit." He pulled a switchblade from his pocket and jostled the release button. A blade shot out. He put it against Jonas's throat. "Let's just see how talented you are."

Jonas's eyes shifted towards Butcher. "Whatever you like, Edmund."

Butcher's smile crumbled. "What did you say?"

"That's your real name, isn't it? Edmund Rodrigo. Grew up in the Philly burbs. Your father was an alcoholic. Not just piss water. Rock-gut whiskey. And your mother. She had her own issues. All those weekend visits to Aunt Maggie's house in upstate New York turned out to be little more than selling skin to feed a cocaine habit."

Butcher looked over at Diggs who stood across the room, arms crossed and amused.

"Little Edmund," said Jonas. "You never liked that name, did you? Can't say I blame you. It has the ring of a pansy. Kids at school teased you. It made you angry. Hateful. Remember that time you poured lighter fluid on a garbage sack stuffed with kittens? You tossed them over a bridge. That made you feel strong. Powerful. A natural born killer. That's what you're thinking now, isn't it Edmund? That frightened little boy feels rage. He wants to fight back. Cut my throat."

Butcher's hand shook. He raised his knife and then lowered it again. "That's enough."

"I know," said Jonas. "The truth isn't easy. Ask Jesus. He got nailed to a cross for it. You dropped out of high school." Jonas forged ahead. "Did some time for robbing a liquor store. After parole you met a girl named Katie Nester. Sweet little thing. Naïve. One night you came home piss drunk. Dinner was late. Real men don't tolerate things like that, do they Edmund?"

Butcher's face, stitched with anger, twisted in different directions of anger. "I said enough!"

"You took your belt off. Slid it slowly out of the loops. Felt the leather against your fingers. You beat her, Edmund. You beat her to raw meat. She tried running. Locked herself in the bathroom. You kicked the door down. Minutes later she was draped over the toilet, bleeding and gasping. You weren't done though, were you? You ripped her blouse off. Threw her down on the cold linoleum. Had your way with her. Fucked her. Then you killed her." Jonas's eyes shifted to Emma and then back to Butcher. "Is that what you're planning on doing with this one?"

A gust of heat rushed through the cellar, almost as if a fan blowing hot air blew on Butcher's face.

Butcher looked over at Emma and jumped back. Instead of a rookie CIA operative, a ghostly vision of Katie Nester sat curled in the corner of the room. Strawberry blonde hair, matted with blood, hung down the middle of her forehead. Her blouse was shredded. A black blister marred her jawline. Tears mixed with dirt and blood raced down the corners of her sunken and bruised eyes.

"You killed me, Edmund," she said. Lifting her arms, her wrists were cut down to the bone. "Rot in hell!" she screamed.

Butcher's cheeks turned crimson red. He raised his knife high in the air.

"I'll kill you again!" he shouted and rushed forward.

Diggs grabbed his arm and pulled him back. Butcher breathed hard. Sweat poured off his temples.

"Snap out of it!" Diggs shook his shoulders.

Butcher shook his head. He looked around like a man waking from a nightmare.

Diggs looked at him and grinned. "Seen enough?"

64

World Wonders

Butcher rubbed sweat off his neckline. He looked around as if searching for a ghost.

"How did he do that? I saw..." Butcher stopped, recalling the haunting vision of Katie Nester.

Diggs leaned against the wall. "I told you. He has a gift. He knows how to get inside people's heads. Almost sounds like a damn science fiction novel. Imagine the damage someone could do with that kind of power. That's what you're paying for, right? Blackheart isn't a gypsy with a tent on a boardwalk. He's the missing link."

Emma looked at Diggs. He stared back with cold, unmovable eyes.

"There is no virus, is there?" Emma asked. "There never was. You engineered this entire thing. You told Butcher we were coming. Gave away our position. Got everyone killed. This is all about getting Jonas Blackheart. It's all about money."

Diggs pulled a cigarette out. Lighting up, he blew a plume of smoke in the air. "Espionage," he said. "It sucks sometimes."

"You won't get away with it," she said.

Diggs laughed. "Really? There won't be anyone left to tell the story. I'll be the lone survivor. No witnesses. You'll be dead.

Maybe worse than dead. The terrorists, or pukes as I like to call them, no offense," he nodded at Butcher, "might keep you locked up in some shit prison in Afghanistan, eating bugs for breakfast.

"You're also wrong about the virus," said Diggs. "It got stolen from an Atlanta research laboratory last year. I should know," he boasted. "I'm the one who took it. You see? It all works out. Jonas gets captured but the government gets their virus back and averts a worldwide plague. I get twenty million from the radicals and praised for heroism after fighting off the bad guys to the very end. I'd say that calls for a retirement to Fiji for the millennium.

Turning to Butcher, Diggs said, "My part of the deal is done. I wanna be paid."

Butcher tapped a finger on his rifle. "You know where the pickup point is." He looked over at Emma. "What about her? You expect me to babysit a CIA agent?

"Kill her for all I care after I'm gone, but right now? She's the only thing keeping us alive," said Diggs. He walked over to Emma and yanked her head up by the hair. "You hear that Jonas? Any tricks and your fuck doll gets her throat slit."

Jonas didn't answer. He stared mutedly, straight ahead.

Hatred layered Emma's expression. Diggs used her. More than used her. He threw her into a gas stove and lit a match. She twisted her wrists in the rope again. There was no give.

"Time for me to go," said Diggs. "I'll leave you and Jonas alone to get better acquainted." Hesitating, he said, "You know, I admire you, Emma Locke. I read your case files. I know about your past. You were brave as hell back then. Unfortunately, heroism doesn't always pan out. It's a shame, really. Under different circumstances? We might have had something together." His hand shot out and grabbed Emma by a clump of hair. Bending down, he kissed her forehead and then spit on the floor. "Good luck. You're going to need it."

Unscrewing the lightbulb in the ceiling rafter, he and Butcher went up the cellar steps and slammed the door shut.

65
Ties that Bind

The darkness loomed solid as a black wall that gave no perception of depth. Seated beside Emma, she heard Jonas breathing. A faint trace of his outline shadowed the room from a pale stream of moonlight sifting through the window.

Emma couldn't see Hollister. Still, she sensed his lethargic presence. His unmoving body, the elephant in the room, lay at her feet with a bullet impacted in his skull.

"Peaceful, isn't it?" Jonas's words were steady. Almost serene.

She didn't have to see him. She could hear the madness in Jonas's voice. If the lifeboat sank, he'd take in salt water until his lungs turned still. The future was irrelevant. Whether they lived or died didn't matter. Their dire circumstance was an insignificant vehicle that drove them to un uncertain conclusion.

"You never finished your story," Jonas said, his voice haunting the dirty walls. Emma felt his breath on her cheek. "Seventeen," he said. "A tender age. That was the night of the lions and the sheep, and the sheep got slaughtered."

"Stop," Emma said firmly, wrists twisting in rope. "We don't have time for this. We need to find a way out."

Jonas's quiet laughter, a devil in the dark, occupied every corner of the lightless room.

"I disagree," he said. "We have all the time in the world Agent Locke, or at least what's left in it. There're bigger fiends than me or Diggs in the world. The one you have to worry about is buried in your mind. I suppose that's true of most of us, isn't it? People dig deep holes. Bury their past. Those things that are too painful to look at we chose to forget. Love. Hate. Even murder," he said. "You can only keep something like that buried so long. Weeks. Years. Sooner or later the weeds come up. They strangle everything around them. That's it, isn't it? You're being choked by the past from the inside. Ghosts are floating in your head. They'll never stop, not until you find the truth."

Emma could feel Jonas's eyes boring into her, unraveling her secret world. In some twisted way, he was right. Maddy never quite stopped breathing in the recesses of her tortured mind. She couldn't remember what happened that night, at least not all of it. Flashes of her past sometimes ignited the corners of her mind; fire flies lighting up and then just as quickly turning dark.

"You keep bringing this up," she finally asked. "Why don't you just admit it. It was you that night when I was seventeen."

Hesitating, Jonas said, "You really can't remember, can you? It's a drifting fog. That makes you a person without a past, and without a past, there is no future or present, is there?"

Jonas's weight shifted. His shoulder pressed against hers. Emma tried pulling back but her restraints wouldn't allow for distance. Dark or not, Jonas's presence rose like a storm in the desert. She could sense the cellar growing hot again. He was rubbing sticks together. Making a spark. Lighting a fire that led into the dismal recesses of her forgotten world.

"It's time, Emma Locke," said Jonas. "Time for you to go back to the night of the wolves. A time when life was younger. More innocent. As it turned out for you, deadly."

"Jonas," Emma's voice grew faint, distant, even in her own head. She tried to speak but her words trailed off. She was falling again. Falling through space. Through years. Her limbs floated. Drifted in some elapsed chasm of time.

Emma blinked. She swore she saw a white rabbit run past her. It scurried down a hole that magically opened in the middle of the dirt floor. A bright light spewed from it.

"Follow the rabbit," Jonas whispered in her ear. "Are you listening, Emma Locke? Go into the light, deep into that long-forgotten world. Find what you lost. Go now!" his voice cracked.

A whooshing noise blew in her ears, opening a door to her invisible past. Suddenly she was there again.

Part 4
THE VISITORS

66
When the Night Comes

Thump.

Emma Locke lifted her head off the pillow. Her eyes shifted around the bedroom.

Light from an alley streetlamp spilled in through summer curtains. Across the room, Maddy lay twisted on cotton sheets. Her soft breathing somehow made the world a quieter place.

In the living-room downstairs, a squeaky wheel spun in Milo's hamster cage. The steady hum of the refrigerator purred in the kitchen. It was near midnight.

Someone stirred in the next bedroom. The hall light flicked on. Emma's father walked by. Barefoot, a white tee-shirt hung out of his pajama bottoms. Floorboards creaked as he descended the stairway. Standing at the top of the stairs, Emma's mother pinched the fleshy part of her hand.

"Do you see anything Sam?" Sharon Locke asked.

After a minute, "Think it's just the wind." He came back up the stairs and whispered, "Quiet. We'll wake the kids."

Sharon peeked in her daughters' room. Emma closed her

eyes as if sleeping. Satisfied, her parents returned to their bedroom and closed the door.

———

Snuggling her head on a pillow, Emma's eyes dimmed and she drifted back to sleep. Visions of Jake Russo, the Italian boy up the street with the curly dark hair, danced in her dreams. She had a crush on the kid since the 4th grade. In the dream, they walked along the midway at the West End Fair. Buttery kettle corn and the smell of chocolate fudge lingered in the air.

Emma nestled her head against Jake's shoulder on the Ferris Wheel. Afterwards he tossed basketballs at a game stand for prizes.

"A winner!" A carnival attendant dressed in a red plaid shirt tossed Jake a stuffed bear.

Grinning shyly, Jake handed the bear to Emma. He leaned over to kiss her and...

Thump!

———

Emma's head jolted off the pillow. She sat up on bent elbows. Scanned the room. She again looked at her sister. Maddy's soft breathing continued playing against the bedroom walls.

Another noise caught her attention. Muffled voices. She climbed out of bed and quietly pattered down the darkened hall. The door leading into her parents' bedroom stood ajar. Peeking in, she abruptly stopped. Chills tingled her spine. Her feet froze to the carpet.

Two darkened silhouettes stood near the rear of the bedroom. One wore a tattered gray hoodie. The other cradled a sawed-off shotgun in his arms. Both men wore ghostly white masks with painted blood lines coming from the slits at the mouths.

Seated on the edge of the bed, hands at their sides, Sam and Sharon Locke trembled.

One of the intruders raised his shotgun to Sam, eye level. "Who else is in the house?"

"Nobody," Sam answered, a bit too quickly.

"Bullshit. I saw pictures downstairs. Kids."

"They're staying at a friend's house."

"They?"

Tears rushed down Sharon Locke's cheeks. "For God's sake. Take what you want and leave."

The intruder bent down on one knee. He slid a hand over Sharon's exposed thigh. Her leg muscles stiffened. Shivers, cold as an Arctic chill, rushed over her.

"No talking," the intruder warned. "Worse things are in the world than a shotgun blast to the jaw." Craning his head around, he reached over and picked a picture up off the nightstand. "Your daughter?"

Sharon said nothing. Her hands fidgeted.

"You're gonna talk to me." The intruder squeezed her cheeks in his fingers. "I swear to God you're gonna talk." Releasing her, he stood up and wiped a runner of sweat off his neck. Pulling at the mask, he lifted it off his face.

"Drake!" his partner yelled. "You crazy, man? She can see you!"

Smiling ferociously, Drake put the mask back on.

"Listen." He nudged Sharon with the barrel of his shotgun. "Your daughters are here. I'll find them. Tie them to a post. Strip them down and ride all night while you watch. Afterwards?" Drake pulled a knife out from underneath his belt. "I'll slit their throats, ear to ear. Understand? I'd suggest you cooperate."

Hysteria enveloped Sharon's pale exterior. She opened her mouth but her words fell silent in a black hole of terror. A single tear escaped the corner of her eye. It weaved down the side of her cheek.

"Please," she finally said. "They're only children."

Drake grinned. Lifting a hand, he unexpectedly slapped the woman hard across the face. A trickle of blood ran down the side of her lip. He looked over at his partner.

"Crash," he said. "Find them. I need them alive."

67
The Smell of Fear

Emma shuddered. There was no time to think. Move or die.

Barefoot on the carpet, she hurried back to her bedroom. Tiptoeing over to Maddy, she put a hand over her sister's mouth. Maddy gasped as she looked up.

"Don't say a word," Emma whispered, heart hammering. "Someone is in the house. We need to hide."

The door from her parents' bedroom creaked open.

"Hurry," she said.

The walk-in closet in the corner of the bedroom was cluttered but in reach. Pulling at Maddy's arm, they got inside. Summer clothes hung on wire hangers. Flipflops and blankets along with board games were stacked on the floor. The girls scrunched down in the back of the closet. Emma pulled a large quilt over them.

Leaning tight against her sister, Maddy shivered.

"I'm scared, sis. I'm scared deep down in the bones," she said, trembling far too much to go unnoticed.

"Stay still," Emma begged, holding her sister's hand tight.

Footsteps stopped in front of the bedroom door. Leaning forward, Emma peeked out. A darkened silhouette, haunting as a ghost, stood motionless at the doorway. A knife hung from his right hand. The blade glinted dully in muddy light. A stink of cigarettes and whiskey hung in the stagnant air.

The intruder flicked on a flashlight. The dull beam danced across the walls and posters of teenage heartthrobs. It stalled on a table next to Emma's bed. Walking over, he picked up a cell phone that sat atop a Girl's Life magazine. Dropping it on the floor, he crunched it under his boot.

Emma's heart pounded.

A deafening silence, colder than a graveyard on a winter night, fell over the room.

"Little ones," someone whispered. "I know you're in here. I can smell your sweat."

Maddy squeezed Emma's hand harder.

The intruder took a step towards the closet. He looked in at the racks of clothes hanging on a metallic bar. Using the tip of his knife, he pushed the clothes aside with one quick swish. The flashlight beam probed the walls. It stalled on a lumpy quilt on the floor. Reaching in, he grabbed a corner of the blanket.

68

Who's that Knockin'

Knock-Knock-Knock.

The intruder stopped cold.

"Crash," his partner, Drake, called in a whisper from the bedroom down the hall. "We got company."

Crash released the quilt. He stood up straight and walked to the second-story window. Two cops were on the back porch. One shined a flashlight around hedges and a swimming pool in the yard.

"Shit!" Crash said under his breath.

Drake stepped out of the bedroom down the hall. Sharon Locke was in front of him. The barrel of his shotgun sat squarely under her chin. David Locke stood just ahead of them, hands in the air.

"The place must have a security system." Crash's eye twitched nervously.

"What about it, David." Drake tightened the barrel on his wife. "Is the place wired?"

David shook his head tensely. "No."

Another knock. Louder this time.

Drake turned to David. "Here's what you're gonna do. We got pigs loose in the farmhouse. You're gonna get rid of them.

Easy, right David? Don't be a hero." He yanked Sharon's head back, exposing the thin lines of her throat. "You'll be a widower. I'll do the same to your daughters when I find them, get it?"

Trembling, David nodded.

Drake slapped his cheek. "I'll be listening from the top of the steps. Move."

———

David walked downstairs, trudging in bare feet over the cold linoleum. Two police officers with stern jaws flashed their badges on the other side of the kitchen door.

Gulping down fear, David opened up.

"It's after midnight," he said. "Is there a problem, officers?"

One of the cops glanced at sweat puddling up on David's forehead.

"Sorry for the intrusion," the cop said. "I'm officer Pierce. There's been trouble in the neighborhood. We're checking the area."

"Trouble?"

Officer Pierce hesitated. "Hill's gas station. The attendant is dead. Not to alarm you but someone cut his throat. We're doing a house by house check. Mind if we come in and look around?"

David's fingers tightened on the door handle. "That's not necessary. I mean, it's late. I got kids. Don't wanna scare them."

Officer Pierce looked down. He noticed David's hands trembling. "You sure you're okay?"

David paused. Forced a grin. "We're fine."

Hesitating, the cop said, "Keep your doors locked. If you

hear or see anything suspicious, call us immediately."

Nodding, the cops walked down the driveway and around the corner.

———

Drake came down the steps, gun riding Sharon Locke's neck.

Crash hurried to the window. He peeked out from behind the curtains.

"Think the cops bought it?" he asked.

"They better," said Drake. He turned to David. "You got rope in the house?"

"What?"

"Rope, asshole. No speak English?"

"Some... some in the pantry," David said shakily.

Crash walked over to the cold-room and opened the door. Digging around, he found a coil of rope and some silver duct tape on a shelf. There were also cotton balls beside a box of Captain Crunch cereal.

"Got it." Crash held the stuff up.

"Gag and tie them," said Drake. His shotgun hovered over Sharon Locke's head.

Crash pushed David and Sharon into the living-room. He ordered them to lay face down on the floor. Jerking Sharon's head back by the hair, he stuffed cotton balls in her mouth, oily from his sweaty hands. Picking up the duct tape, he unraveled it over her mouth and around her head, then hog-tied her ankles and wrists. Dragging her across the carpet by an ankle, face down, he deposited her next to a coffee table. Finishing the job, he did the same to David.

Propping a foot up on a desk chair, he admired his work.

"What now?" asked Crash.

Drake found an open bottle of wine on the kitchen counter. Unscrewing the lid, he took a swallow. Red dribbles dabbed the corners of his latex mask like fine runners of blood. Jostling the bottle in his hand, he walked to the bottom of the staircase.

"We're not done here," he told his partner. "The kids are hiding upstairs. We need them."

On the living room floor, Sharon Locke left out a quiet but frightened sigh.

Drake glanced over at the woman. His eyes hung there for a minute like hardened cement. He couldn't break the view of her pink ruffled nightgown. It bunched up along her leg, exposing a milky white thigh.

Walking over to David and for no reason, Drake kicked him in the stomach with a steel tipped boot. David groaned miserably.

"That's a fine-looking ass you're married to." Drake took another slug of wine. "I'll give it to you straight, David. Political correctness never was my strong point. The dragon hasn't been out of the cage in a while." He reached down and fingered a swell in his trousers. "With your permission I'd like to screw your wife. I'd be honored to have you watch." Drake removed his belt.

David's eyes rolled up. Rage overtook rivers of terror. He breathed hard through his nose. His wrists twisted furiously in knotted yellow rope.

Crash walked in the room and stared dumbly. "Are you crazy? Cops are everywhere, man. We got to go and..."

"Shut your face." Drake pointed the shotgun. "You'll get your turn."

Sharon's eyes shattered in dread. Drake rolled her over on her back like a slab of beef. He kneeled down but abruptly stopped at the sound of loud, shattering glass. Quickly standing up, he moved to the bottom of the staircase and scanned the stairsteps.

"It's the daughters," Drake said. "Get them. Now!"

69

Hide and Seek

Maddy clung around Emma's neck. Fat tears rolled down her cheeks.

"Don't leave me sis." She trembled. "Please don't leave me."

"I promise I won't. You'll be safe. I have to see what's going on," Emma whispered. "Stay quiet. If someone comes, stay still." She squeezed her hand. "No matter what happens, don't come out."

Nose running, Maddy nodded with big wet eyes.

Peeking out of the closet, Emma crawled across the carpet on hands and knees. For an instant she thought about screaming. Maybe attracting the police's attention but it would be more a cry of suicide than redemption. Cornered animals fight. The intruders would kill everyone, including themselves, rather than be captured.

Outside the bedroom, the hall was empty. Tempting fate, she crept to the top of the staircase. She could see overtop a wooden railing that led into the living room. The sight struck her like an iron plate. Both of her parents were on the floor, tied and gagged.

The big one, Drake, walked by the steps. Ghostly white latex mask casing his face, he glanced up the staircase. Emma quickly mortared herself against the wall.

In the other room, there was a loud thump followed by a sickening groan when he kicked her father in the ribs. He then approached her mother. Took his belt off. Got down on his knees.

Emma's mind whirled in blades of terror. The bastard was going to rape her.

Shifting her vision left, a table stood in the hall. A glass vase filled with geraniums sat on top. Emma grabbed it. Hesitating less than a second, she smashed the vase against the wall. Glass sprayed everywhere.

Footsteps quickly moved to the bottom of the stairs.

"The daughters," she heard Drake say. "Get them."

———

Emma raced back into the bedroom. A sliver of glass from the broken vase clipped the heel of her foot. Biting down hard, she kept moving.

There was no time to get back in the closet and get under the quilt. Footsteps already sounded out from the staircase. Quickly hitting the floor, she rolled under the bed and stifled her trembling limbs.

Craning her neck to see, Emma peered out from underneath the bed frame. Scuffed boots stood at the bedroom's entrance. Crash again, she thought. Tapping the edge of a knife on his trousers, he took a step forward.

"No noise. Don't even breathe. Please Maddy," Emma thought. "For God sake, stay quiet."

Finally, Crash turned and headed up the hall but abruptly stopped.

The sound was faint. Almost inaudible. Quiet whimpering came from inside the closet.

Emma's heart froze. Crash's fingers tightened on the knife. Back peddling, he reentered the bedroom. He glanced at a picture of Jesus hanging on the wall, briefly hesitating as if contemplating the consequences of his actions. Finally, he walked in and opened the closet door. Hinges squeaked.

"Well now," he said, reaching in.

Eyes bright and damp, Maddy refused to stand up. She balled into a fetal position on the carpet, hands jammed into her armpits. She let out a loud, deafening cry as Crash pulled her out and picked her up.

"Crash?" Drake called from downstairs. "Cops are around. Shut that kid up!"

Crash's dirty hand slapped tight over Maddy's mouth. Limbs thrashed as he tucked her tightly under his arm. He waved the blade of the knife in front of her.

"Stop it," he warned.

Maddy blinked uncontrollably. Her breath rose and fell in quick raspy pants.

"Where's your sister?" Crash asked sternly.

Maddy said nothing. Faint sighs of terror escaped her windless chest.

Crash craned his head around. He studied the darkened corners of the room.

"I'll be back," he warned. Tucking Maddy under his arm, he exited the room and down the staircase.

70

Bat Girl

Emma's fingers dug into the carpet.

"Maddy," she whispered quietly, nearly in shock.

Rolling out from underneath the bed, she looked around the bedroom. Trying to subdue Crash in hand to hand combat would have been suicide. The intruders were stronger. Deadlier. She needed a weapon. Hairbrushes were on the night table. Teen magazines. Maddy's dolls sat on a cedar chest. Still, nothing to use as a formidable defense.

A sudden spark lit the corner of her mind. Her father kept a baseball bat in the spare bedroom, just down the hall. He said he used it back in the old high school days to knock one over the fence. That's what she needed to do. Bang it out of the park, only instead of a ball, the target settled on the bony exterior of her assailant's skull.

Mustering courage, she stood up and crept down the hall, careful to avoid shards of glass from the broken vase. Muffled voices talked downstairs. Drake and Crash. They were arguing about something.

Emma slipped into the spare bedroom. The wooden bat was propped against a wall, next to a box of Christmas ornaments in storage. Picking it up, she slid her fingers tight around the handle.

71

Desperate Measures

Maddy's legs dangled from under Crash's arm as he trotted down the staircase. The young girl's eyes amplified in terror at the sight of her parents tied up on the floor.

"Found this hiding in a closet," said Crash.

Drake stared. "Where's the other one?"

"She was alone."

"Shit she is. We need to find her. You wanna get paid?"

A police car went down the street. Crash gripped the sink counter. "Can't we get out of here? You killed that guy at the gas station. Slit his throat. Cops are everywhere."

"You're stupid, right?" Drake said. "Everything is sealed off in a ten-block radius. We need to hunker down. Let things cool off."

Crash eyed his counterpart. A shotgun hung tensely in his hands. He looked shaky. Unstable. Still, Drake always had a plan. Not this time though. He went ballistic at the gas station.

———

It was a chance meeting over at a low rent bar in Freehold. Drake said he was going to pull a job. He said it would pay big money. He told Crash that he wanted to hire him for a night.

Fresh out of jail and unable to find work, Crash complied.

Later that week, they were on the road. Drake pulled into a self-service island for gas. Talk about déjà vu. A felon, Chuck Pagosa, recognized Crash from back in prison. He started spouting off about how Crash turned him in on a parole violation. Chuck threatened to tell the cops they were there. That's when the worm turned.

Drake went nutzo. He pulled out a switchblade and rammed it into Chuck Pagosa's throat until it scraped bone. The convict dropped to the macadam, twitching and jerking under a neon sign. A woman in the parking lot screamed. Drake hurried back in the car and peeled out.

———

A few miles down the road, Drake pulled over in an alley.

Opening the glove compartment, he tossed Crash one of the latex masks that he bought in a costume store on 42nd street. The disguises were white. Bony as malignant spirits with bloodlines painted down the sides of the mouth.

"Keep this on." Drake slipped the mask over his head and looked in the rearview. Sniggering, he said, "We'll look like drag-queen terrorists."

Crash looked dumbfounded. "Are you crazy? You killed that guy at the gas pumps. We got to get out of here."

Drake had a mad twinkle in his eye. It was that "don't fuck with me" look.

"Shut up," he warned. "Once we're done, forget you were ever here. I'll see that you get paid in full. I'll even get you a lift to

Mexico."

The next thing Crash knew, they jimmied a lock and busted in a house.

———

"What now?" Crash fidgeted.

Drake grabbed a piece of candy out of a dish. He unraveled the paper and popped it in his mouth, sucking at it with his lips. Walking over to a trashcan, he tossed the paper away.

Crash stared.

Crazy, man. Drake just committed murder. People were tied up and gagged in the living room. He was worried about littering the floor.

Staring, Drake walked over to Maddy, who shivered on the couch. Too terrified to speak, she trembled nonstop. Grabbing a handful of cotton balls off the coffee table, he stuffed her mouth and then lassoed the duct tape around her head. She struggled to breathe through a runny nose.

Afterwards, he pulled a picture of two kids off the living room wall. They were smiling. At a zoo maybe, next to a statue of a giraffe. He tossed the picture to Crash.

"Find the other one," he said. "We need her alive. After that, we'll figure out our next move." He stepped over to the window and stared into the darkness. "We need to be gone before daybreak."

72

Swing Away

Emma heard footsteps coming up the stairs. Her limbs stiffened into iron plates.

Peeking out from behind a door, the dull beam of a flashlight skittered over the walls. It was the smaller one again. Crash. He turned left, towards her bedroom. She heard things being overturned. Maybe a night table or a lamp. Then it got quiet.

Emma's muscles tightened. Her fingers scrunched the stem of the bat. Her toes scrunched into the carpet as if standing on a trip wire, ready to detonate.

It was futile to hide. He'd find her. When he did, he'd punish her all the harder. She considered crawling out the window and shimmying down the drain pipe. However, if the thugs believed she escaped and went for help, there's no telling what they'd do to her family.

Rather than be cornered, she opted for ambush. Catch the intruder off guard and take him down. Half the terror would be eradicated.

Listening closely, it got quiet. Crash might have detoured into the attic, thinking she hid up there.

Tempting fate, Emma stepped into the hall. She saw no evil shadows lurking in the dark.

"Crash?" Drake yelled from downstairs.

No answer and no surprise. Crash decidedly didn't want to compromise his position.

Fearing that Drake might come and investigate, Emma hurried down the hall. She detoured into the bathroom. A slow steady drip sounded off in the basin of the sink.

Emma crinkled her nose. A rank smell assaulted her senses. Whiskey, mixed with the stench of perspiration. Even worse, she heard breathing. It came from behind the shower curtain.

Emma whirled around. The curtain flung open. Crash stood there boldly. This time instead of a knife, he wielded a gun. Emma swung the bat hard. He partially blocked the blow with his arm but the wood reverberated in her hands as she partially connected with Crash's cheekbone. A sound like hardened snow crunching under a boot cracked the silence.

Crash groaned loudly. Staggering backward, he dropped the gun and gripped the shower curtain for support. Emma quickly reached down and scooped it up.

"Don't move!" she shouted in a loud voice.

Blood seeped on Crash's mask from around his ear. He got to his knees and slowly raised his hands.

"Take it easy," he told Emma.

"I said don't move!" The gun trembled in her hands.

From downstairs, Drake yelled, "What's going on up there? Crash?"

"She's got the gun," Crash hollered back. His fixed gaze never wandered from Emma.

A quiet pause and then, "Tell her to come to the top of the

steps," said Drake. "You listening darling?"

Terrified but holding steady, Emma inched her way to the staircase. She never lowered the weapon from the cruel eyes behind Crash's latex mask. Glancing down the steps, she froze.

At the bottom of the staircase, Drake held her mother. A knife probed her throat. Inaudible whimpers of panic escaped from underneath her gag.

"Pay attention, sweetheart." Drake tightened the blade on Sharon Locke's throat. A thin line of blood hung on the edge of it. "I'll slit and gut your mama like a fish. Drop it."

Fear shadowed Sharon Locke's haunted eyes as she watched her daughter. Emma knew that look. Her mother was gentle but also courageous.

Sharon Locke suddenly dropped straight to the floor. The knife nipped her neckline but Drake became an open target for an unguarded moment.

Finger's trembling on the trigger, Emma took aim.

"Die!" she abruptly screamed and fired.

The shot thundered through the house just as Crash crept up and hit Emma from behind.

73

Captured by the Moment

Emma woke up on the couch. Her wrists were bound in rope but unlike her parents and sister, she wasn't gagged or her ankles tied.

Shifting her eyes to the bottom of the staircase, a jagged hole cut through the drywall. There were no signs of blood. When she fired, she missed.

A frightened moan made her turn. Maddy sat beside her on the couch. Tied and bundled, her eyes shifted fearfully from side to side.

In the next room, her mother lay face down on the floor. She looked at Emma but fear alone didn't leak from her eyes. She nodded ever so slightly as if to say, "You can do this, Emma. Don't worry about me. Save yourself. Save Maddy. You can make it out of here alive."

Heavy footsteps lumbered up the pantry steps in the kitchen. Crash, his skeletal white mask glowing in a faint light, was dabbed with blood from where Emma hit him with the bat.

"Got the Oldman tied up in the cellar," he said. "Stone walls and dirt floor. Freaking place looks like a morgue."

Drake sat on a recliner in the living room, tapping his

finger on the shotgun. He craned his head towards Sharon Locke.

"Her too." He motioned to Crash.

Crash walked across the room. He grabbed Sharon by the ankle. Like a hunter dragging a fresh kill out of the woods, he pulled her across the rug. Sharon's eyes briefly met Emma's as she passed. Thumps and groans rang out as Crash hauled her down the cellar's rickety staircase.

"Shut up!" Crash's voice drifted up from the basement, followed by the sound of a loud slap.

Sucking wind, Crash came back up the stairs. He grabbed the wine bottle off the kitchen counter and took a slug and then angrily smashed it against a wall.

"What are we even still doing here, man? That kid fired the gun. Someone had to hear it. We got to get the hell out."

"Can it," said Drake.

"But..."

"I said shut up!" Drake shifted the barrel of the gun in Crash's direction.

Crash took a step back. Drake was losing it. Sometimes he did that. He got tremors. He'd shake all over as if a demon was trying to punch through his skin.

Drake got up and marched across the room. Emma squeezed her eyes shut as if unconscious. The intruder's towering presence, well over six foot, magnified tenfold by the white ghoulish mask covering his face.

"I know you're awake." He leaned in close. Emma smelled the stink of his sweat. Grabbing her hair, Drake yanked her head up. She gasped and opened her eyes.

"What's your name?" he asked.

"Emma," she answered, looking him squarely in the eye.

"We ran out of rope and tape." He glanced at her ankles. "Don't let that influence you. Run and I'll kill your sister. Simple, right?"

Trembling, Emma nodded.

"Any guns in the house?" asked Drake.

A cold chill crawled over Emma.

"Answer!" he ordered and held up his hand.

"No!" She turned her head, bracing herself.

Drake lowered his hand again. He looked at Maddy. Her limbs shook. Tears flooded her eyes.

"I know," said Drake. "She's special. Young. Innocent." He reached over and held Maddy's trembling chin with greasy fingers. "You're gonna cooperate with me Emma. If you don't..."

"Don't touch her!" Emma blurted out.

Defiance was met with a hard slap across the mouth. A red bruise instantly swelled on her cheek.

"Anything else to say?"

Emma swallowed hard.

"That's better." Drake stood up. "We got a long night ahead of us."

74
Thinning the Herd

Crash paced the kitchen floor. Opening the refrigerator, he found a can of Bud Light and popped the cap. The beer dribbled down the corners of his mask. Crunching the empty can, he tossed it on the floor.

"This is nuts," he said. "Let's get out Drake. We've been made. We can still make it to the border."

Drake stared out the window as if in deep thought. Turning around, he glanced in at Emma and Maddy.

"The parents," he said in a whisper.

"What?"

"In the bedroom when we first got here. They saw my face," said Drake. "You know what that means." He set the shotgun down on a table in front of Crash.

Crash stared at the weapon. "You want me to kill them?"

"They'll identify us. We can't take that chance. You hate knives, right? Too close and personal. The cellar is underground. It should absorb the blast. If the cops didn't come when the kid fired off a round, they sure as hell won't hear that."

Crash backed up and raised his hands. "You wanna kill them, go ahead. This is getting freaking crazy. I'm out of this, man."

Drake's fists stiffened. "You going sour on me Crash? We

killed someone at the gas station. What do you think the cops will do if they catch us?"

"You killed him," Crash said. "Not me."

"Doesn't matter," said Drake. "In the end? We'll both ride the lightning." He walked to the top of the pantry steps. "Those people down there? They'd love to see us hang. Even worse," he said. "They think you don't have the balls to do it. They're laughing at you. Mocking you."

Crash turned away and gripped the kitchen counter. "I'm not killing anyone."

Drake walked over and grabbed Crash by the shirt. "What the hell kind of a partner did I team up with? We'll get out of here after you do it. Get our payday. Maybe fake some passports and be on a beach in Belize before the week is out. Lots of beer. Women." Drake looked at the cellar steps. "Not if it's up to them though. They'll get us locked up in some shithole on death row until we get 2,000 volts in the chair. You gonna take that from them?"

Crash's hands shook. Sweat dripped off his neck. He reached for the shotgun but pulled back and lowered his head.

"Pussy," Drake said, pushing Crash away. "Let me show you how sheep get slaughtered in a meat house."

Grabbing the shotgun, Drake turned and disappeared down the stairsteps.

75

Things that go BOOM in the Night

Dark rivers of terror washed over Emma. She heard arguing in the kitchen. Something about killing them. She saw Drake, the bigger of the two, glance in the room to see if she was listening.

Her wrists were raw. Still she found that after twisting around, the rope loosened. Gritting her teeth and with one last tug, her hand squeezed through the knot.

In the kitchen, Emma heard the bolt of a shotgun being drawn back.

Clump, Clump, Clump.

Heavy boots descended down the cellar steps.

An avalanche of fear caved in on her. She touched Maddy's arm, mouthing the words, "Don't make a sound."

Emma got up. Tiptoed over to the dining room table and picked up a brass candleholder; a present for her parents' twentieth anniversary. It was heavy. Solid. She crept to the kitchen doorway. Crash stood at a counter near the sink.

In the cellar, sounds of ripe terror emerged from underneath her parents' gags. It filtered up the stairwell.

Crash turned just as Emma sneaked up behind him. She

swung the candleholder hard but Crash blocked it with his arm. Pulling it from her, he flung it across the room. It smashed against some glasses in the sink.

"I told you." Crash bundled her in his arms. "Stay quiet."

More sounds of dread in the cellar. A silence followed, sharper than a winter morning with snow falling on a deserted side street.

"Mom?" Emma struggled to free herself from Crash's grasp. "Daddy?"

One second. Two seconds. Three seconds and then...

BOOM!

Another second.

BOOM!

The horrific moans that hung restlessly in the warm night air stopped cold.

"No!" Emma screamed and dropped to her knees.

76

Cleaning up Loose Ends

Drake trudged back up the cellar stairs. He tossed the shotgun on the kitchen table.

Crash stared at the pantry door. The elephant in the room just doubled in size.

"Crazy sonofabitch. You really did it?" he asked.

Drake looked at Emma. She kneeled on the floor, hands covering her face. In the other room, Maddy struggled for breath, her heart outracing a fuselage of fear.

Letting out a fierce cry, Emma lunged forward. Drake greeted her with a firm backhand, knocking her back to the floor.

Even Crash looked shaken. He wiped a greasy strand of hair from his face. "Let's just get out of here."

Drake hesitated and tilted his head. "We're not done," he said, glancing at Maddy in the other room.

"You're joking, right?" asked Crash.

Drake stood stock-still. "Two hostages are too hard to handle. I only need this one." He glanced down at Emma.

Crash pointed a finger. "I'm not killing kids."

"What's wrong with you?" Drake grabbed Emma by a clump of hair and lifted her head, her eyes wet with tears. "She's just like this one. She'd stick a knife in your heart if you give her the chance. We're taking our little friend Emma with us. We'll use her in case things get ugly," he said. "But the other one? Just like the parents. She's disposable. We'll load the bodies in the car. Head north. Weight them down and dump them in a lake. Nobody will ever know."

Crash said nothing. Drake stared at him with contempt.

"What' wrong?" Drake picked up the shotgun and shoved in Crash's hands. "You afraid?"

Crash shifted his gaze to Emma, who looked back with pleading eyes.

"I'm not scared of anything but I'm not killing anyone."

"Don't do it Crash," Emma suddenly spoke. "He wants you to kill her. That makes you both guilty."

"Shut your face!" Drake said, slapping a hand over Emma's mouth. "If you don't do it, there won't even be a trial. The police will kill us. Is that what you want? Take the shotgun. Finish it."

Crash shook. "I can't just..."

"Do it!" Drake pounded a fist on the kitchen table.

Hesitating, Crash slowly turned towards Maddy in the other room.

Fear swallowed Emma like a shark in dark waters. She tried wriggling free. Drake's grip was too strong.

"On three," said Drake. "Pull the trigger. She dies and we're home free. One," he counted. "Two."

Crash stepped towards the living room. He raised the gun. Aimed it at Maddy. She squirmed uncontrollably on the couch.

"That's it," Drake said. "Ready?" He paused. "Three!"

Crash squeezed the trigger but a sudden disruption rocketed through the kitchen window, shattering the glass. A bullet caught Crash dead in the side of the neck. He hung there for a frozen moment, staring forward. A look of surprise fell over him as he lifted his hand to his neck. Gawking at the blood on his fingers. he fell to the floor.

77
Lights

Bright lights lit up the outside of the house. Holding tight to Emma, Drake ducked behind the refrigerator. Another bullet plunked in its metal exterior.

Three feet away, Crash's limbs twitched on the linoleum. He tore off his mask revealing a man, mid-twenties, with a brutish and sweaty face. Finally, his body stopped shaking and turned cold.

Drake put a knife to Emma's throat. Dragging her along, he maneuvered over to the shattered window. A shadow ran across a garage roof on the opposite side of the alley. Someone else hid behind the neighbor's swimming pool. Police cruisers enveloped the house.

For a fleeting moment, Drake considered suicide. Stick the barrel of the shotgun in his mouth. Taste the cold steel and hot bullet within. That thought dissipated when another spray of glass shattered the remaining portion of the window. Someone tossed a cell phone inside. It landed in the sink on some dirty dishes and began ringing.

Knife wedged under Emma's chin, he reached up. Fishing it out of the sink, he hit the talk button.

"This is Lieutenant Wayne Andrews. Who am I speaking to?"

Drake remained silent.

"The house is surrounded," Andrews said. "There's no way out. Give it up. Nobody has to get hurt."

A stark vision of Sam and Sharon Locke's cold remains in the cellar flashed in Drake's head. If he didn't end up on a joyride via the electric chair, he'd be locked up in some rathole for the millennium.

No thanks. No fucking thanks.

"You gonna cooperate?" asked Lieutenant Andrews. "Your partner is shot. You'll be next. You want that? I don't think so." Andrews answered his own question. "You got my word. No gunfire. Send out the hostages."

Drake grinded his teeth fiercely. The last thing he needed was some wiseass cop calling the shots. Sweat discharged from Drake's pores. He grew nauseous. A vile taste erupted in his throat but he pushed it back down. Pulse racing, he surveyed the outside world. Police had all exits covered. No doubt the roads leading out of town would be choked.

Reaching down, he took the shotgun out of Crash's lethargic fingers and placed it against Emma's neckline. Ducking behind her, he lifted her head into full view at the window.

A rookie cop who was ducked behind a police cruiser fired off a round. Emma screamed as the bullet landed a yard away in a wooden porch railing.

"Hold your goddamn fire!" Lieutenant Andrews yelled.

Drake said over the cell phone, "About that name. You can call me Drake and this is bullshit. You think I'm stupid? You'll open up the minute I walk out."

Lieutenant Andrews stood there motionless. His tie flapped

in the warm July heat.

"Here's what's gonna happen," said Drake. "Call your dogs off the roofs. Anyone makes a wrong move, this kid is gonna be talking to angels." He shook Emma by the neck. "Now back off. I'm coming out."

78

Lieutenant Andrews

Stars shined brilliantly in the summer sky. Chained to a coop down the road, a neighbor's dog barked. It was a normal evening that was anything but ordinary.

Police lights sparkled off Lieutenant Andrews' face and illuminated the exterior walls of the house. Lieutenant Andrews looked at the cop standing beside him.

"Who's in the house?" Andrews asked Officer Hess.

"The guy's name is David Locke," Hess said. "Married. Two daughters."

"What about the perps?"

"We got a glimpse of the one we shot after he removed his mask. His name is Clay Metzler, better known as Crash," he said. "Freaking guy was a programmer who went ballistic and nearly killed someone. Recently paroled. A badass but no murder raps.

"No idea who the other guy is," Hess continued. "All we know is he calls himself Drake. Probably an alias. Maybe a drifter."

Lieutenant Andrews stood there, his mind fogged in an impenetrable haze.

It was a small town. Hell, boring was the word. Parking tickets or an occasional drunk who grew a set of balls and started a fist fight were the extent of a busy Saturday night.

The call came down, fierce as a demon. There was trouble over at Hill's gas station. Someone got his throat cut. By the time the ambulance arrived, blood and petrol ran down the parking lot. The victim stared lifelessly up at the fluorescent overhead lights of the self-service island. An APB and two hours later, shots were fired in the vicinity of Mulberry Street. No houses were around but a woman walking her dog heard the blast. It came from the Locke residence.

Behind Andrews, Channel 16 News rolled up the road. They tried crossing the police line.

"Get them back!" Andrews shouted. "We got kids in there. I don't need some whacko getting antsy."

Tension creased Andrews's forehead. He dabbed at his face with a handkerchief and stared at the house with impenetrable eyes.

"Who's your best sharpshooter?" he asked Officer Hess.

"Lyle Mantz, hands down. He's on the garage roof, directly across the street."

Lieutenant Andrews scratched at beard stubble. "Tell him to be ready. The moment he gets a shot, take it. No maiming or long court trials. Bury him, understand? Also keep the radio clear. He might have our frequency. Go," he said hurriedly.

———

Five minutes passed.

Ten minutes.

Lieutenant Andrews checked his wristwatch.

"We got movement," a cop to the left of him said.

Lieutenant Andrews looked up. A mechanical door from the house garage rolled up. A car idled inside, hi-beams on.

Lowering his eyes, he honed in on a transmitter clipped to his suit jacket.

"Mantz, you with me?" Andrews asked, lips barely moving.

"Right here, Chief," Mantz said from atop a toolshed across the alley.

"You got a shot?"

Mantz hesitated. "Too much glare from the headlights. I can't see a damn thing."

Andrews crunched his fists. The cell phone in his hand started ringing. He put it to his ear.

"Hello Lieutenant. Just a confirming call. I'm not sure you take me seriously, but wouldn't want you to doubt my veracity," Drake said. "Go to the kitchen window."

"What?"

"You heard me asshole."

Gulping, Lieutenant Andrews walked slowly up the driveway. Pale violet lilacs traced his steps in the yard. He squinted from the blinding headlights of the car in the garage. He cautiously walked up on the porch. Flicking on his flashlight, he shined it in the broken window.

Stuff was strewn around. Blake Metzler, alias Crash, lay on the linoleum. His hand still clutched at his throat from where the bullet entered.

Moving the light across the room, Andrews gasped and gripped the porch railing. Two more bodies were in the room. One was slumped up against the refrigerator. The other, a female, had been spread eagle on the kitchen table. Both were gagged with a gaping hole in their heads.

"Any of this resonating with you, Lieutenant Andrews?" asked Drake. A tickle feathered his voice. The sonofabitch was enjoying it.

"The daughters are with me," he said. "Turn off the spotlights. First sign of a hero they'll be joining mommy and daddy, get it? Now get back."

79

The Exodus

Blood receded from Lieutenant Andrews' cheeks. He backed away from the house and glanced at the transmitter hooked to his suitcoat.

"Mantz," he said quietly.

"Yes sir," he answered through an earpiece Andrews wore.

"Stand ready. You need to nail this bastard."

"Got you," Mantz answered.

Lieutenant Andrews turned to the troops. "Turn the spotlights off. Lower your weapons!"

Confused police officers wearily stood down. Flashing strobes and headlights all went dark.

The car, a black sedan, shifted forward and a rolled slowly down the driveway.

"Mantz?" Lieutenant Andrews said under his breath.

"Sonofabitch!" Mantz's staticy voice crackled in Andrews's earpiece.

"Talk to me," Andrews said. "He got the hi-beams on. We can't see anything."

"He got pillows stacked up on the rear window. Sheets are stuffed in the sides so you can't look in."

Lieutenant Andrews stiffened. He looked at the dark

exterior of the car "What about the windshield?"

Mantz hesitated. "No good. He has a blanket covering him and the kids. Looks like they might be all bunched together in the front seat. That's one smart killer. I can't get a clear shot," he said and then, "What you wanna do?"

Lieutenant Andrews stood there stone-faced. He was screwed. Three cold kills, two more potential murders and his hands were dipped in cement. No way in hell could they let this guy escape. Still, opening fire would finish what Drake began. The cops would kill all of them.

After a minute, "Hess," he said to the cop beside him. "Tell the men to hold their fire. This bastard won't hesitate to pull the pin if he thinks we're gonna nail him. We already have all the exits blocked going out of town. Get cops planted everywhere in a ten-block radius and beyond. Keep them hidden. If he smells a tail, game over."

Officer Hess nodded and hurried away.

The black sedan continued down the driveway. The pace was slow. Deliberate. As if to remind Lieutenant Andrews just who was in charge, the car nearly came to a dead stop next to him before continuing on down the road and out of sight.

80

Trail Blazing

Peering out from behind a crease in a quilt, Emma gripped the steering wheel. The barrel end of Drake's shotgun rode the undercarriage of her chin.

Seated on Drake's lap and nightgown ruffled up, his cruddy jeans felt damp against Emma's naked legs. A hint of urine hung in the air. It occurred to Emma that Drake might have pissed himself.

Maddy was gagged and tied on the passenger seat. She rested against Emma's thigh and shivered. Sobs of distress filtered up from underneath a layer of duct tape.

"Turn up the alley. Circle left," Drake tightened the gun on Emma's neckline.

Emma's eyes were frozen and untraceable. Hours ago, she dreamed about kissing the cute boy next door. Like a nor'easter barreling up the coast, that quick she became an orphan in a cold world of terror.

At the top of the backstreet, Emma veered left towards the interstate. She couldn't tell if the police followed. Drake had the windows sealed tight with pillows and blankets.

"Down that road," he said, rancid breath swamping Emma's nostrils from underneath the blanket.

Emma turned the wheel.

The road wasn't a road at all but a trail that led into a wooded area. Maneuvering the vehicle was difficult. It bounced off rocks and potholes. About a mile in, the path widened and opened into a field surrounded by trees. Tall grass blew hauntingly in the wind under a thousand sparkly stars.

"Pull over and shut the engine off," Drake ordered.

Emma hit the brakes. A distant siren, police scouring the night for a killer on the loose, cracked the darkness.

Drake finally took the blanket off them. In the light of the moon, his white mask, a ghost disfigured as melting wax, appeared even more ominous.

"Get out of the car," he ordered Emma. "You know the deal. Run and I'll kill your sister." He yanked Maddy's head off the passenger seat. Her eyes were canyons of terror.

Emma slowly exited the vehicle. A lazy summer breeze brushed her hair. Woods grew thick on both sides of the trail. It was secluded. Barren of houses. Remnants of a campfire sat at a clearing on the side of a path. A few dented-up Budweiser cans littered the ground. Probably teenagers who stole a few cold ones from their parents' refrigerator.

Drake hoisted Maddy out of the car. He carried her over to a dead tree stump and plopped her on the ground beside a crib of weeds. Pale and sticky as wet paint, her face dripped with distress. Curling up in the dirt, she pressed her elbows against her sides and whimpered quietly, nose sniffing and running.

"Sit down." Drake pointed at a rock beside Maddy. "Stay quiet and you stay alive."

Emma lowered herself to the ground. Her gaze never

shifted from the shotgun aimed between her eyes.

Another distant siren made Drake stiffen. He looked from left to right, clearly unable to determine a means of escape.

Emma leaned over and rested her shoulder against Maddy. She nodded quietly, urging her sister to remain still. Drake was faced towards the woods. Reaching down, Emma picked at the rope lassoing Maddy's ankles. After three tries, she managed to uncoil the loops. The knot slipped open.

Drake turned and Emma froze. He eyed her suspiciously, then turned his attention back to the surrounding area.

Emma looked around. Maddy's legs were loose but escape seemed impossible. Drake had a shotgun. He wasn't afraid to use it. He'd mow them down in a heartbeat.

A loose rock in the dirt sat not more than a few feet away. If she could lure Drake in close, she might be able to grab it. Hit him hard enough to stun him and make a run for it. Dense woods fenced the perimeter. If they could get to the tree line, they could disappear in the forest. Hide until help arrived.

Limbs stiff as iron, Emma silently waited.

81

Mystery Callers

Drake looked around the dark edges of the woods. Keeping a careful eye on Emma, he pulled a cell phone out of his pocket and placed a call. Someone picked up.

"That's bull," Drake said angrily in the phone. "You said there wouldn't be any glitches. Easy pickings." He paused. "Crash is dead and I got cops crawling up my ass. There's no way out."

Another siren wailed in the distance.

Drake flinched. The entire job turned to mud. It would be a miracle if he didn't get cornered. There would be no trial or sentencing. He'd be on the front line of a firing squad before sunrise.

Drake heard Maddy cough from underneath a mask of duct tape. He looked over at her. The kid didn't look good. Probably the gag or a ball of cotton got stuck in her throat. Lugging her around wouldn't help matters. He needed to move fast if he wanted to stay alive. She'd slow him down.

"Listen," Drake said, gripping the phone. "I got two kids with me. I can't lug them around and make it out of here alive."

There was a long pause on the phone. Drake listened intently to whoever was on the phone. After a minute, he clicked the phone off and shoved it in his pocket. He again turned his head towards Maddy. The girl shifted against Emma's shoulder. Panic eroded her heart and fright swam in her eyes. She again tried to cough but her breath beat against a wall constructed of duct tape and cotton balls.

Drake's untiring stare remained fixed on the young girl. He appeared to be waiting, almost as if suffocation rather than murder would end the problem by itself.

Tapping his foot slowly, he stood up straight as if coming to a firm decision. Glaring maliciously, his fingers tightened around the shotgun.

82

A Wolf in the Darkness

Emma's face was a cross nailed between confusion and fear. Whoever was on the phone, judging by Drake's responses, it wasn't a random break-in at her house. They were targeted.

Maddy gasped under the lining of duct tape, lungs burning from a lack of oxygen. Flower white complexion, she sagged over on Emma's lap.

"She can't breathe," Emma blurted out.

Drake stared wordlessly.

"Did you hear me!" she said louder.

Maddy started choking. Regardless of Drake's frightening presence, Emma reached up and tore the tape off her mouth. She spit out the cotton balls and gulped air. Looking up at Drake, Maddy let out a stifling scream, loud enough to flutter bat wings in the dark trees surrounding them.

"I told you." Drake raised the gun. "No noise!"

Drake marched forward. An alarm sounded in Emma's head.

"NOW!" it screamed.

Emma reached for a rock with stretched fingers. Grabbing it, she met her assailant's approach by smashing it directly in his face. He stood there, momentarily stunned.

Without hesitation, Emma took hold of Maddy's arm. She pulled her off the ground. Frantically looking from side to side, the woods were close but too far to mount an escape. Drake was already shaking off the blow. He'd kill them before they ever reached the tree line.

Thinking fast, she pushed Maddy into the passenger seat of the car. Hurrying to the other side, Emma jumped in. The keys hung in the ignition. She fumbled them in her fingers. Finally, the engine started.

A loud crash made her shriek as the sound of a shotgun blast exploded the rear window. Glass sprayed everywhere.

Drake raced around the car and nearly vaulted over the hood. He ripped the driver's door open. Emma tried kicking him away but he caught hold of her ankle. Dragging her out of the car, he threw her on the ground.

———

Drake dropped the gun and pulled a switchblade off his belt. He clicked the release and the blade jetted out.

"I told you before. Play by the rules," he said. "You didn't listen. Now there'll be consequences."

Kicking furiously, he pulled Maddy from the car and put the blade to her eye.

Shaking off dizziness, Emma jetted off the ground and leapt at Drake. Knocking the knife from his hand, Emma scooped it up and jabbed. The knife-edge caught the arm of Drake's hoodie. His sleeve grew damp with blood. Standing boldly in front of her sister, she held the knife like a samurai sword.

"Get away!" Emma shouted fiercely.

She again swiped with the knife but Drake grabbed her wrist. Twisting it, the weapon fell to the ground. Instead of back peddling, Emma sprang forward. She got her hands underneath Drake's mask. Her fingernails raked across his eyes and cheekbones.

Drake groaned but then just as quickly hit her hard with a closed fist. Buckling over, she tumbled to the dirt and came to an abrupt stop against a large rock.

Emma's eyes lost focus. The world grew dim and full of shadows. It echoed with the haunted sighs of her sister.

"Sis!" Maddy called. "Help me!"

Emma struggled to her hands and knees. She dragged herself across the dirt and bodily covered Maddy.

Breathing heavy, Drake picked the shotgun up off the ground. He trudged towards them. Raising his boot, he kicked Emma away. She groaned and rolled off her sister.

Drake's eyes were dark slits behind a hideous disguise. Reaching up, he pulled off the mask. Tossing it aside, he spit in the dirt.

Emma struggled to her knees but fell down again. Blinking with unfocused eyes, Drake appeared hazy as summer heat rising off asphalt.

Bending down, he pulled Emma's head up by the hair. His stale breath hung in her nostrils.

"Meet the wolf," he said, almost whispering. "First your sister dies, then you."

Emma gazed hazily. For a moment the lines in her disconcerted mind connected. Drake's face constructed. Dark hair. High cheekbones. Piercing eyes, empty and cold of warmth.

"Help me sis!" Maddy's voice, a distant echo, channeled through her fading thoughts.

Her consciousness adrift into realms of darkness, she heard the sound of a shotgun bolt being drawn back. It clapped like a firecracker in her head.

"No," Emma mumbled, raising her hand in the air.

A gunshot sounded off. The blast resonated in the trees and open fields.

Turning around, Drake stood there. He looked at Emma, a malignant spirit embracing the darkness.

For an instant, Emma's vision cleared. Drake's distorted face shined in moonlight. His penetrating gaze bore down on her. She looked closer. Tried to see and then...

Part 5

SAVING THE WORLD

83

Inside Connections

Emma woke with a hard slap to the face. Butcher stood in front of her. The stark lightbulb socketed into the ceiling rafter hung over his shoulder.

Blinking her eyes, she tried to collect herself. Jonas linked to her a mind again. He took her back to relive her terrors of the past. It was vivid. Intense. Maddy's screams still echoed in her head. The smell of gunpowder lingered in her nostrils.

Emma looked around. She was back in the cellar, tied to a post. Intelligence had ordered her to go on assignment to Area 51. Her and a team of commandos set out to find Edmund Rodrigo, alias the Butcher. The dominos had fallen since then.

Jason Diggs, CIA superstar, had turned out to be a mole. He sold them out and led them into a trap.

"Your friends are dead," Butcher said, circling like a vulture. "You'll join them soon." He stopped walking and stood in front of her. "Diggs is a traitor. Still, he understands greed. He delivered Blackheart and he'll get his money." He paused and stared. "It seems things worked out for everyone but you."

Across the room, Butcher's radio started to hum. He walked over and picked up.

"Diggs?" someone said.

"He's gone," said Butcher.

"Was the package delivered?"

Butcher looked at Jonas. He remained quiet, eyes closed. "We have Blackheart. The commandos are dead. Hell, everyone is dead."

"What about the resident bitch?"

"She's here. Pissed but alive."

After a pause, "Agent Locke?"

Emma looked up. An air or recognition waved in her expression..

"Lanster?"

"None other," Lanster said. "Things are going according to plan but it seems as if you got caught in the net. I hate to see a woman like you get wasted, but business is business. I've got a couple of million riding on this."

Pieces began to fall in place. Lanster signed the release papers to get Jonas out of Area 51. He was working with Diggs, conspirators till the end.

"You'll never get away with this," Emma said.

"Darling, that bridge has already been crossed." Lanster sniggered. "Diggs just called in a Code Red to headquarters. Right now, a group of New York's finest are headed to Soho. They're converging on room 212 of the Tower Apartments. All eyes are on New York instead of the real action. Agent Caskie is heading up the operation. Good for him. I never liked that bastard. While they're out busy chasing their asses, Diggs is collecting our ransom money.

"By morning, Diggs will emerge as the lone survivor from the mission," he continued. "He'll turn over the virus that he stole from the CDC in Atlanta. Intelligence will hail him as a hero. They'll search through the casualties. You and Jonas Blackheart will be missing. They'll assume you were captured by the hostiles but it won't matter. The virus will be secured. The world will be safe again, all because of Diggs. Even if those idiots at Intelligence find out the truth, by that time we'll be hidden away on some island in the South Pacific, drinking margaritas on the beach.

"As for you?" Lanster paused. "It's time to say arrivederci. I understand you'll be bunking in some shit prison in Afghanistan with the rats. Don't worry," he said. "It's a matter of time before your usefulness runs out, along with your life. My guess is you'll be counting the days."

Restraints dug into Emma's wrists as she shifted forward. "Lanster," she said. "Diggs is crazy. You'll never get whatever he offered you. He'll disappear. Lanster!"

———

Butcher clicked off the radio. "Enough games." He pulled a syringe out of his pocket. Turning, he walked over to Jonas. "This won't hurt. By the time you wake up you'll be in a tucked away in a rathole, somewhere in Kabul." He bent down on his knees and smiled. "I want you to know something. I'm not gonna kill your whore. I still have men in the field. They had a long night. Could use some downtime. Call it stress relief." He winked at Emma. "She'll moan until sunrise, tied to a rafter and rode like a mule, over and over. Afterwards? If you behave, I might let her live. Cross me? She'll be peeled open like an orange."

Butcher tore Jonas's ragged sleeve away. He put the syringe to his arm.

Jonas's eyes opened and slid towards him. "I wouldn't do that, Edmund."

Butcher tilted his head in amusement. "And why not?"

Jonas grinned. "Because my hands are free."

Letting out a gut-wrenching cry, Jonas ripped his arms from the post. The beam nearly cracked as the rope snapped off his wrists. He grabbed Butcher's arm. Twisted it. Butcher shrieked as Jonas flung him to the floor. Moving in, a tiger on the hunt, he wrapped his hands around Butcher's throat, squeezing and twisting, almost as if unscrewing the lid on a rusty jar. Fingers clenched, he jerked his head to the right. There was a loud pop, almost like a bubble bursting. Butcher's mouth flapped open lifelessly, his dead fish eyes staring at the ceiling.

Breathing heavily, Jonas pulled a knife from Butcher's belt and turned to Emma.

84
Killing the World

Jonas's chest heaved. Emma watched his slow approach; a malignant spirit coming to feed. For whatever reason, a memory of eating ice cream on the boardwalk in flipflops flashed across her mind. Her mother and father were there. Maddy skipped beside them, singing a song. It was the last summer vacation they took together before that terrible night of the murders. Judging by the look on Jonas's face, she'd be joining her family again soon.

"It's your time, Emma Locke," said Jonas, gripping the knife.

Emma squeezed her eyes shut and readied herself.

Reaching behind her, with one quick swipe, Jonas cut the rope from her wrists.

Exhaling, Emma stood up slowly. Her gaze never wandered far from the man in front of her.

Jonas said, "I suppose Intelligence never prepared you for things like this. It's just me and you now."

The prophetic words struck Emma like a cold slap. It was true. Training educated her on how to endure and survive in hostile environments. Still, no drill could ever prepare her for the realities staring her in the face. She looked down at Butcher's cold remains, his eyes forever slanted in regions of terror.

"Do you know what you've done?" She looked up at Jonas. "Butcher was the only person who knows where Diggs went. If he decides to use the virus, you just killed the world."

Jonas leaned against a wall in a dark corner of the cellar. "Simple twists of fate happen every day." He turned from left to right, listening to the silence. "It seems strange, doesn't it? No bangs or screams. I believe T.S. Eliot said it best The world quietly goes away in a whimper. Much like poor little Maddy, you couldn't stop it."

Emma bent down. She found her Glock stuffed in Butcher's trousers.

"Shut up," she said, raising the weapon.

Searching further, she found a lighter. Switchblade. Even a stick of gum. Finally, she came across what she was looking for. Pulling her cell phone out of his back pocket, she punched in a number.

———

"Agent Locke?" A staticky voice answered. "It's Jeff Sterner over at command."

"Sterner, I need help," she said. "I'm..."

"We know where you are," he cut in. "Intelligence gave us the lowdown on your operation. What the hell is going on over there?"

"There's no time to explain." She looked at Jonas. "Everyone here is dead."

Sterner sounded confused. "We just got a call for a Code Red from Agent Diggs. He said the target is at an apartment in Soho. We've got a team headed there now."

"It's a setup," said Emma. "The target isn't there."

"A wave of static came over the line. "You still there Locke?" asked Sterner.

"Diggs and Lanster are moles," she forged ahead. "Can you hear me?"

More static, heavier this time.

"Sterner?" Emma said. "Sterner!"

Sterner's voice disappeared in snow.

85
The Tower Apartments, Soho
2:10 a.m.

Amidst Soho's artist lofts, art galleries and trendy upscale boutiques, the Tower Apartments sat in the center of town. It took less than twelve-minutes for federal agents to reach the building. Agents dressed in everything from white protective suits with oxygen masks to AC/DC tee-shirts surrounded the place. Snipers positioned themselves on rooftops opposite the veranda of room 212.

Agent Caskie, an investigator with a plump gut and gray mustache jabbered on a radio.

"You reading me?" He glanced up at room 212. The curtains were closed, lights on. "Everyone is in position. We're ready to blow the lid."

"You got the perimeter sealed?" someone asked on the other end. "This bastard slips through the cracks, we're toast."

Agent Caskie again looked around.

The call came in less than an hour ago. Jason Diggs. He said something about a highly toxic material at an apartment in Soho. Caskie wasn't far away. They'd been there ever since.

On the perimeter, men hid in hedges and on fire escapes. Alleys and highways were barricaded. Across the road, two undercover detectives posing as hippies with tie-dyed shirts and baggy jeans leaned against a parking meter. The only difference from them and street bums were the semi-automatics hidden under their shirts.

On the roof of the veranda outside of room 212, Special Agent Manny Greer crawled spider-like on a tin canopy. Nope. This guy wasn't walking out of the place under his own power.

"We're set to go," Agent Caskie said over the radio.

———

Special Agent Manny Greer crouched down on a large canopy above the terrace. Footing was poor and even less sturdy. The rusted tin crackled whenever he moved his shoe.

A warm wind ruffled Manny's brown curly hair. It was one of those nostalgic Soho nights in lower Manhattan. As a teenager he remembered taking a girlfriend to the Villa East Cinema. What was her name? Natalie Prat. Yeah, that was it. She was the *IT* girl back in the college days.

He moved his foot slowly. Tin crunched again. What the hell was he doing here? Instead of those sweet romantic nights from long ago, he readied himself to crash through a window and subdue an imminent threat. The real kick was that he volunteered for the mission.

Manny smiled. "Man, I'll do anything for a headline."

A few clicks back he headed up a raid on the Mexican border. Some drug runner had a brick of C4 strapped to his chest. He threatened to blow himself up. It never came to that. Agents opened fire and popped the cork themselves.

This was different.

Greer saw snipers in trees. Street cops in plain clothes meandered the sidewalks. That was routine. The real kicker was that a task force from the CDC had taken up residence. Men in white suits and breathing apparatuses sat in an armored vehicle behind a garage at the rear of the apartment complex. It had to be toxics. Maybe even nerve gas.

"Life on the edge," he muttered and took another step on the canopy.

Instructions were clear. An agent posing as the nightshift manager would knock on the door. If they didn't open, he'd kick the sonofabitch down. That would be the signal to bust through the veranda's window. Orders were to shoot anything that moves.

"Keep your respirators on," the chief told them. "The minute the place is clean, there'll be a vehicle waiting outside. You'll be taken to quarantine for observation."

Sweet. Real sweet.

Manny reached in his shirt pocket. He pulled out a picture of his wife and daughter. Kissing it, he stuffed it back in his fatigues. A noise suddenly hummed in his earpiece.

"Greer," said the chief. "We're green on Dragonfly. Lock and load."

86
Operation Dragonfly

Special Agent Nester Reed ambled up the hall towards room 212. He was a seasoned veteran for twenty years. Seen some major caca go down in his days. Extorsion. Drug busts. Even a senator sniffing cocaine with a hooker in the Bronx. His orders were crystal. No survivors, period.

What frightened him more than the prospects of an automatic machine gun was the respirator covering his mouth and nose. Bad air sucks. Especially the kind that kills you.

Walking quietly to the door, Reed listened. Adrenaline pumped like firewater in his veins. A television played a familiar tune. Gilligan's Island, for God's sake.

"Reed," the chief said in his earpiece. "You in position?"

"Ready," he whispered in a mic attached to his shirt.

After a moment of hesitation, "Engage."

Reed raised his knuckles to the door and then lowered them again. The hell with that. Gritting his teeth, he whirled around and busted the lock with a firm kick. The door flew open on broken hinges.

Gun cemented in his hands, he burst in the room. Nobody was in sight. He tossed a gas bomb across the floor. Smoke fizzed up. Still, there were no signs of a target. He did, however, hear something in bedroom. Someone was laughing.

———

From out on the veranda and boots first, Agent Manny Greer crashed through the terrace window. Glass exploded everywhere. Finger bolted on a trigger, he sprayed bullets in all directions.

"Come!" Greer shouted.

A squad of agents, goggles and breathing apparatuses attached, piled in the door.

Pivoting from left to right, Greer yelled again. "Reed! Where the hell are you?"

Tear gas smoked the rooms. Greer turned and headed down a hall that led to the bedroom. Looking in, he stopped cold. Agent Reed stood there staring at something.

A rocking chair sat in the corner of the bedroom. A doll was seated on it. The figurine's mechanical lips opened and closed in a hearty laugh. Ticking evenly, a timer was attached to its silicone body. It counted down from twenty seconds.

"Get out now!" Reed shouted.

Agents clamored for the exit. Time, however, wasn't on their side.

With one final tick of the clock, the room detonated.

8₇

The Killer on my Shoulder

Emma looked blankly at the radio and then up at Jonas, gun riding between his eyes.

"You told Sterner everyone was dead," Jonas noted and glanced at the gun. "Does that mean I'm going to the afterlife?"

Emma said nothing. She stared coldly, never lowering her eyes. The gun barrel remained fixed on the target, safety off.

"What's wrong. No taste for murder? Go ahead," Jonas taunted. "Do your worst."

"Don't tempt me Jonas," Emma warned.

"I suppose it all begins now, doesn't it?" said Jonas. "People are out living their lives. Lovers are holding hands by the ocean. Others are sleeping. Maybe making love to their wives or putting children to bed, all the while the world hangs in the balance. None of that matter though, does it Agent Locke?" He looked at the gun again. "You have an agenda of your own."

Emma met Jonas's gaze. "You don't need to be a mind reader to know that."

Jonas grinned. "Is that any way to speak to an old friend?

You should have seen yourself that night long ago. So heroic and noble. You couldn't help your family though. It doesn't matter how much time goes by. You can't stop the screaming in your head. You're here to exorcise ghosts. You know what ghosts are, don't you Agent Locke? Demons from the past. Monsters that lurk in the dark recesses of people's minds. You can't forgive yourself for what happened that night. It eats at your insides. Swarms like maggots feasting on dry bones. Still there's no changing things. Fate, you know. It always has its way."

Silent rage pressurized in Emma. "Before this night is over, it'll have its way here."

Emma stared at Jonas, his eyes marble and lifeless as a shark hunting in dark waters. He didn't have the charisma of a glamour killer like Bundy. Jonas dismantled his prey psychologically, piece by piece.

"I want the truth," Emma finally said. "The night my family got murdered. Were you the man in the mask?"

Jonas tilted his head coyly. "What do you think?"

"Stop!" she shouted. Hot tears glistened her eyes. She stood up. Put the gun to Jonas's head. "Don't you know what that did to me? How it felt to listen to the cries of people you love begging for mercy just before the bullet hits. For God's sake. Didn't you ever care about someone, Jonas? Maddy was a little girl. Never went to a dance. Never put on a prom dress." Emma tightened the gun on his temple. "Never had a chance to live, you sonofabitch."

Jonas felt the cold steel of the gun probing his damp skin. Emma's finger trembled on the trigger.

"You've finally found it, haven't you," said Jonas. "The killer on your shoulder. That madness inside. You want to shoot.

Release the hate. Feel the pressure lift." He paused. "I suppose this is where it all ends."

Emma stood there, eyes unwavering. "Then die," she said, her finger squeezing at the trigger.

Jonas suddenly blurted out, "Broadway."

Emma froze. "What?"

"Intelligence in all their brilliance is looking for the virus in places like New York. Talk about idiots, I give you the CIA."

"What are you saying?" asked Emma.

"Diggs doesn't have the virus hidden away in some rickety apartment in Manhattan. It's here."

Emma tilted her head. "How do you know that?"

"I'm a mind reader, remember? I saw it in Butcher's mind, just before I cracked his neck," he said. "The operative holding the virus is in town. Believe his name is Conner but people refer to him as Sharky. Not sure why but I gather it isn't a pleasant story. He's waiting for Diggs."

Emma stared. Could it be possible? All the while Intelligence blanketed New York, the virus sat in a small northeastern town, minutes away.

"You're lying," Emma countered.

"Am I?" Jonas shifted his eyes to the gun pressed against his head. "Pull that trigger and you'll never find out."

After a minute, she withdrew the weapon and looked out the darkened window.

If Jonas told the truth, getting a hit team dispatched in time was impossible. Diggs would be gone before they ever arrived. If he decided to do the unthinkable and use the virus, it would carry fast as dry leaves in a windstorm.

Emma looked over at Jonas. He smiled playfully.

"Tick, tick, tick." His finger swayed back and forth. "Time is running out."

88

Homecomings

Emma drove down the wooded path. Jonas sat beside her in the passenger seat. The van rocked over potholes until they turned right on a darkened highway. Driving with one hand, she held a gun on Jonas with the other.

It took only minutes to reach Jim Thorpe, a town named after an old Indian athlete. Old Victorian houses sprang up on both sides of the road as they entered. Streets were vacant at that late hour.

Jonas smiled. "This must remind you of that night long ago. Dark. Cryptic. Only this time instead of your sister, the entire world rests on your shoulders."

Emma ignored him.

"Are you sure this is the right way?" she asked.

Jonas turned his head and looked at a dark mountainside in the backdrop. Nostalgia dripped in his eyes. "Trust me, Agent Locke. You might call this a homecoming. Some people refer to it as the six degrees. Any two people are less than six acquaintances away from knowing each other. I've been here before."

The van moved slowly down the road. Antique shops and coffee houses dabbed the street. It was the perfect weekend getaway rather than a stage set for the end of the world.

"Pull over." Jonas pointed.

Emma parked next to a pizza shop and cut the engine. It was nearly 3:00 a.m. A bartender from the Molly McGuire's pub locked the front door and meandered up the street. A few lights speckled tenement windows. For the most part, everyone was asleep.

Jonas looked up at an open window on the second floor of a building, next to a record shop. Curtains blew in a warm wind.

"That's your destiny, Agent Locke," Jonas said. "Imagine the implications. The rookie CIA agent with the murdered family takes on the greatest case in American history. If you fail, the world goes with you."

Jonas's words swirled in Emma's head. Even now he tried to make her uncertain and unguarded. She picked up a cell phone and started to punch in a number.

"Stop wasting time." Amusement caked his face. "It would take at least an hour for reinforcements to arrive. You, on the other hand, have minutes."

Emma lowered the phone. It was true of course. By the time a team was assembled, even by chopper, it would be too late.

Thinking fast, she pulled handcuffs out of the glovebox and tossed them to Jonas.

"Put them on," she ordered.

Jonas didn't move. Emma raised her Glock.

"Don't test me," she warned.

Jonas laughed out loud. "Don't tell me you're that naïve. You can't shoot. Even silencers go pop. Our friends might hear. They'd know you're coming." He stuck his head out the window and sniffed the night air. "It's a beautiful evening. A little wet but clean. Fresh." Opening the car door, Jonas stepped out. "It's your time, Emma Lock. The night of the jackal. The moment you've been waiting for all your life. Go. Save the world."

"Stop." Emma extended the gun. "I swear I'll kill you."

Jonas smiled. "Don't make promises you can't deliver."

Opening his arms as if breathing air for the first time in years, Jonas walked down the street and vanished into the night.

90

Sharky

Emma ducked in an alley beside the pizza shop. The stink of garbage from a dumpster baked the night air. Halfway up the side of the apartment building, a security door sat atop a set of cement steps. Its gray exterior had been graffitied with the words, "Eat the Rich". She turned the handle on the door. As expected, it was bolted shut.

A few yards away, a rickety fire escape led up to the second floor of the building. Emma began climbing. Twice her shoe got caught in a rusted hole in the metal. Finally, she reached the second story. Tiptoeing across the landing, she peered into a partially open window. Nobody was in sight.

Emma moved towards a door. She twisted the handle, surprised when it turned. Pushing it open a crack, she peered in. It was dark as midnight.

Glock in hand, she opened it a little further. With nobody in sight, Emma slipped in

———

Light sifted in the window from an outside street lamp. A beat-up chair with worn armrests sat in the corner of the room.

An empty pizza box lay on the floor. Music played from somewhere in the apartment. Jim Morrison and The Doors.

Emma moved slowly through the room. She peeked around a corner into an open corridor that led to the kitchen. An overhead fluorescent light blinked as if ready to burn out. A few crunched beer cans were strewn over a counter near a sink. Someone shuffled around.

Static came from a radio on the kitchen table.

"Diggs, you there?" a voice said from around a corner. "It's Sharky. What the hell is happening? Diggs!" he shouted angrily.

A hesitant pause was followed by a loud thump. Sharky smashed his fist on the kitchen table.

The suspect crossed the room. From Emma's angle, she only got a faint glimpse of him in the muddy light. He was thin but not overly tall. Ruddy complexion. A police baton swung haphazardly back and forth in his fist.

Sharky turned his head towards the open corridor. Emma backed up. Her foot bumped the corner of a chair, making her freeze to the carpet. Seconds later, the music from the kitchen turned off. Thick and hard as cold steel, a suspicious hush fell over the room.

"Diggs?" Sharky called.

Haunting silence.

Suddenly, Sharky smashed the baton against a table.

"Who the fuck is in there!" he yelled.

Emma's pulse raced. Sweat glazed her skin. Her hands stiffened on the Glock.

With a war-like cry, Sharky stormed into the hall.

Emma fumbled with her weapon. She boldly stepped out of the shadows.

"Don't move!" she shouted. "CIA!"

Sharky stopped and stared, almost in amusement.

Emma sized him up. He had long greasy hair and a scruffy beard. A faded tattoo of a skull ran up his forearm. His eyes, soulless and cold, stared through her as if she were plexiglass. He started forward again.

"I said freeze!" Emma warned. "Drop the baton. Now!"

Sharky flipped a string of hair from his eyes. Hints of a smile crossed his lips. He let the baton slide through his fingers and fall on the floor.

"You looking for this?" He held a small flask of up. "Careful. One spill makes a big mess."

Emma's heart jumped. It had to be the virus. The bastard was the carrier pigeon.

"Down on the floor," she ordered. "Hands behind your head. Move!"

Instead of compliance, Sharky turned and bolted the other way. Emma fired. The bullet plunked emptily in a plaster wall. Holding tight to thin reeds of courage, she hurried down the hall in pursuit.

———

Emma stopped at the entranceway of the kitchen. Deafening silence stagnated the air. Still no signs of Sharky. She eyed a door that led to a terrace.

Sharky suddenly lunged out of the shadows. His knife caught her in the arm before knocking her to the floor. He quickly straddled her, putting his weight landed on her chest. Still grasping the flask of poison, he grinned sharply as he raised the knife for a fatal strike.

"Time to say goodbye." He stared brutally.

Emma answered with a kick to the groin. Sharky's confident expression evaporated. He dropped the flask containing the virus. It bounced off a linoleum tile and landed on a rug, still intact.

Kicking him off her, Emma reached across the floor and latched on to her gun. She swung around and fired at point blank range as Sharky swooped in on the attack.

Stopping cold, Sharky hung there for a long moment and then fell to the floor.

Sweat washing Emma's face, Emma pulled herself to the edge of the couch. She touched her shoulder. It was wet. Sticky.

"Bleeding," she said, her head woozy.

Emma looked around the unlit corners of the room and blinked. She heard another noise. A darkened silhouette stood in the archway.

91

A Rose in the Weeds

Moonlight from the window hung over the stranger's back. A grin cemented his lips. Jonas walked towards her.

"You finally saved the world, Agent Locke. Maybe little Maddy will rest easier in her coffin tonight."

Emma pushed herself up on bruised elbows and looked through half-lidded eyes.

"Why?" she asked.

Jonas lifted an eyebrow. "Why what?"

"It was you, wasn't it? You killed my family."

Bending down on crooked knees, Jonas picked up Sharky's knife. He tapped the blade with his finger.

"You still don't remember, do you?" he said. Leaning over, he set the knife back down beside her. "We both have our passions. Yours is to find the killer who murdered your family. All those long years rotting away in a dank prison, mine was to find you. I remember the terror in Maddy's eyes that night. I remember you," he said. "All those years of sitting in prison, you were like a rose growing among the weeds in my mind."

"I don't understand," Emma said.

Jonas paused. "You were your sister's hero. Her superman. She counted on you. Believed you'd protect her. Save her. I saw that in her mind before she died. You tried to keep her alive but couldn't. All these years it tore at you like old denim. Now here we are, face to face, and you still can't see the truth."

Reaching over, he pushed matted hair away from her face. "It's time to meet the monster, Emma Locke," he whispered in her ear.

A familiar heat, hot as a desert baking in July, rolled through the open spaces of the room.

Emma's skin felt warm. Clammy. Like before, she began to drift to another time, one that took her all the way back to an empty and deserted road when she was seventeen years old.

92

The Man behind the Mask

As if her spirit separated from her body, Emma floated. Her ghost hovered over the scene of the crime.

moonlight shined off the hood of a car coming up a woodsy path. It came to an abrupt stop in a small clearing. A man with a white ghoulish mask exited the vehicle.

"Out of the car," he said in a gruff voice. "Run and I'll kill your sister."

Emma watched herself get out of the vehicle. The man in the mask pulled Maddy off the passenger seat. He carried her to the other side of the clearing and roughly set her down beside some rocks.

Maddy coughed. A choking noise escaped her from beneath a bed of duct tape.

"She can't breathe," Emma heard herself say.

The man said nothing. Gripping a shotgun, he stood there, fierce eyes behind a white latex mask.

In a bold move, Emma yanked the tape away from Maddy's mouth. Maddy coughed wildly, followed by a shrieking scream.

The masked man angrily started forward. Emma's fingers fumbled in the dirt. She grabbed a rock buried in some weeds. Hit him as he approached.

Pulling Maddy to her feet, she ran for the car. Fumbled with the keys.

A loud shotgun blast exploded the car's rear window. It sprayed glass everywhere. The masked man flung the car door open. He dragged both of them out. Tossing the shotgun, he pulled a switchblade off his belt. The blade jetted out.

"No!" Emma screamed.

She lunged at the masked man. He dropped the knife. She picked it up and frantically swiped the air.

"Get away, you sonofabitch!" she yelled fiercely.

The masked man caught Emma's wrist. He twisted it as she stabbed. Emma dropped the weapon but lunged forward. Fought him. Fought him hard. Scratched at his eyes and cheeks.

Grunting, the man in the mask hit her hard with his fist. Emma gasped and tumbled backward. Her head plunked off a rock. She shook it groggily. Dragging herself across the dirt, she cradled Maddy in her arms, covering her up.

The man stood there, his presence merged in darkness. He trudged forward. Kicked her. She groaned. Rolled off her sister.

Sucking at the warm night air, the man reached up and pulled his mask off. He leaned down and grabbed her by the throat. Stared at her, eye to eye. Wind played in his hair, bending it like stalks of wheat. His boyish features were overpowered by his dark eyes, cut into blades of hate and rage.

Emma held her breath. The person's face struck hard as an anvil.

"You," she said breathlessly.

93

Hellraisers

Emma woke up on the floor. The room temperature cooled down. Whatever Jonas did to lead her back to that terrible night, it was gone.

Still, she sensed she wasn't alone. Over by the archway. Someone walked across the room, a forgotten demon from the past. He wore that same ghostly mask that haunted her years ago. Red bloodlines painted its bony exterior.

"It was you," Emma said.

The dark figure pulled the mask off. He tossed it on the floor next to her. She recoiled at the sight of it.

"I kept this as a souvenir." he said. "I always figured one day you'd remember."

Emma took a long breath. "Diggs."

Diggs nodded. "That would be Jason Drake Diggs to you."

———

"You killed my family," Emma said. "Why?"

Diggs kept his gun on her. "I was a hellraiser in those days. I worked for The Agency. They were the same people who created Jonas Blackheart. Specialized in telekinetic research. Believe it was called Operation Jackal back then. I got hired to do a job, straight out of the academy."

Emma stared. "What job?"

Diggs bent down. "We weren't at your house that night on a robbery." He paused. "We were there to get you."

Emma's face drew a blank. "I don't understand. What would The Agency want with me?"

Diggs smiled coldly. "Because Emma, your entire life is a lie. Nobody made love on a starry beach to bring you into the world. Your mother worked for The Agency. She was a volunteer in a college program. They were testing a new drug that promoted psychic ability.

"Ever wonder why you couldn't find your real parents?" he asked. "The Agency erased the records. Your mother's real name was Annette Sanders. She was a lot like you. Defiant as hell so I'm told. She tried quitting the program. That wasn't allowed. There were consequences. She needed to disappear."

Emma asked, "They killed her?"

"No," said Diggs. "The Agency faked her death. Made it look like she got murdered. They even planted a dead body by a lake and then got one of their cronies to confirm that it was her.

"They hid mommy dearest away in one of their facilities. Did research on her. She got pregnant, not the good old-fashioned way by screwing in the backseat of a Chevy. They did the job artificially. After she gave birth, they told her you were still-born.

"You were put up for adoption," he said. "The Locke family took you in. Raised you. Gave you a good home. Still, The Agency kept watch. Hell, they probably knew what deodorant you wore.

After years, they wanted you back. Maybe pick up on the research from where your mother left off."

———

Emma listened in disbelief. If Diggs told the truth, she hadn't been an orphan left on a street corner. She was a target, accountable for the death of her family."

Emma's fists stiffened. "Where's my real mother now?"

"Who knows," Diggs answered. "She went crazy from the drugs they pumped in her. She's either locked away in an asylum or at the bottom of lake, anchored down by rocks."

"And my father?" Emma said hesitantly.

Diggs grinned. "If you're asking me if Jonas had a daughter, that's a question you'd need to bring up with him."

"Why should I believe any of this?" asked Emma.

Diggs shrugged. "It doesn't matter if you do. My job that night was to abduct you. Make it look like a robbery. Things went sour. The police moved in. My partner, an ex con who needed money, got shot. Didn't matter. He was a pain in the ass. I would have pulled the trigger myself before it was over.

"A few years after the murders you applied for a position at Intelligence. Talk about miracles, I give you the CIA." Diggs laughed. "You never got hired on merit. Intelligence knew about your history with The Agency. They wanted to keep tabs on you. See if you possessed any of those nifty little telekinetic gifts passed on from your peers.

Diggs stared at Emma with carefully scrutiny. "You blacked out that night, long ago. I wondered if it would jar your memory when we met at Area 51. As far as I can determine, our friend Jonas Blackheart did that for you."

Moving closer, Diggs ran the barrel of the gun down the side of Emma's cheek.

"You got in my way, Emma. You let Jonas escape. If I don't deliver him to the radicals, I don't get paid. It isn't all bad," he said. "I'll return the virus and be a hero. The lone survivor in a fight that saved the world from a deadly threat. Sounds like a great headline. Maybe I'll even write a book and go on Oprah, right? The problem is, you're the last witness to the crime," he said. "Years ago, your family saw my face. They could identify me. I'm a professional. I didn't make the mistake of letting them live. I won't make that mistake now, either."

Reaching out, Diggs touched her hair. Emma shuddered as if a bat flew down her shirt.

"I want you to know something," he said. "Your family didn't die easy. I came down the cellar steps that night. I remember them staring at me. The terror in their eyes. Can you imagine what they were feeling? A killer with a devil's mask and a loaded shotgun. They were tied. Gagged. Their eyes begged for mercy. First your father. Then your mother. She cried as I put the barrel to her head. I pulled slowly down on the trigger. Shot them like rabid dogs. Now I'm gonna do the same to you. It's nothing personal. Just business."

He put the gun to her head. "Goodbye, Emma Locke. It's been a pleasure serving with you."

94

Point Blank

A shutter waved down Emma's spine. Her gaze shifted to the Glock. It sat near a heating grate, a few feet away. It would take a miracle to reach it.

"Pleasant dreams," Diggs said and pressed the gun against her temple.

The alarm sounded in Emma's head like an air raid siren.

"Now!" a voice screamed.

Emma rolled left just as Diggs fired. The bullet embedded in a floorboard. Kicking hard, she caught Diggs in the ribs, staggering him backward. Lunging on elbows and knees, she grabbed her Glock off the floor. Twisting around, she fired.

Diggs jerked backward and clutched at his arm. Emma discharged another bullet, this time hitting him in the trigger hand. Diggs dropped the gun but instantaneously tried to pick it back up.

"Don't move!" Emma squared the barrel of her weapon on his forehead.

Disregarding the command, Diggs reached for his gun. Emma fired again, this time taking out a kneecap.

Diggs let out a deep groan and dropped to the floor. His face twisted in sections of both shock and fear but mostly dismay.

He simply could not believe a goddamn rookie was getting the best of him. He reached out and picked something up off the floor.

"Hold your fire!" he shouted. "You know what this is, Emma?" He held the flask up containing the virus. "It's the end of everything. Put the gun down or I'll smash it open. You wanna be responsible for killing the world?"

Hands shaking, Emma held her aim.

"You'll kill the world anyway," she said. "You're crazy, Diggs. Put it down," she ordered.

Diggs smirked.

"Put the fucking thing down!" she shouted.

Diggs stared. Uncertainty washed over his face. He could see it in her eyes. She wasn't a newbie anymore. She'd kill him. Put a hole in his head. He looked towards the door and touched his throbbing knee from where he had been shot. Running wouldn't only be futile. It was impossible.

Surprisingly, Diggs set the flask on the coffee table. He raised his hands. His breath was heavy. Labored.

"It looks like you win," he said, still searching the perimeter for a means of reprieve.

Emma didn't move. She steadied her aim. The smile evaporated from Diggs's face.

"You really gonna pull that trigger?" he asked. "You better think about it first. I'm the most trusted agent in the business. I have classified information that even Intelligence isn't aware of. They won't believe any of your story, Emma. You'll be under investigation. Maybe even prosecuted. It doesn't have to happen that way." He stumbled down on his hands, trying to hold his balance. "Tell them we both survived. We'll find Blackheart. Split the money. That's millions, Emma. Think what kind of a life you could have with that."

Emma's gaze remained solid as diamonds, the target intact.

"Money won't buy back the life of my family," she said. "You killed them, Diggs. Murdered them in cold blood. Someone has to pay for that in the end. There's consequences."

Despite the pain, Diggs managed a smirk. "Then take me to trial."

"You're already here," she said. "I'm the jury."

A cross of both fear and rage swept over Diggs. Suddenly he lunged at Emma. She instantly pulled the trigger. The bullet landed squarely in his forehead. Diggs stopped moving on contact. He slouched to the floor, his blank eyes staring at the ceiling.

Emma fell back on the carpet and dropped the Glock. Hands tingling, she struggled to remain conscious. The world around her echoed with dark chimes; forebodings of her impending mortality. She turned her head towards Diggs who lay dead on the carpet.

"Got you, you sonofabitch," she said tiredly.

Eyes blurred and losing blood, she again looked at the archway next to the window. Another figure appeared.

95

Goodbye Again

"You finally saved the world, Emma Locke." Jonas stepped forward and leaned over her. "You lost blood. I wouldn't worry. You're incredibly resilient. You'll live to fight another day."

Emma coughed. Eyes glazed, she looked up.

"Diggs killed my family. You had to know. Why didn't you tell me?"

Jonas lifted his head. "What justice would that have been? Furthermore, you wouldn't have believed me. Tell me something," he asked. "All these years you've blamed yourself for your family's death. Even now, after saving the world and with the killer dead, you still can't satisfy the hunger of your own guilt, can you? They died and you lived. Tell me," he asked. "Where did it end for Maddy?"

Emma hesitated. "In a hospital room," she said. "I held her hand all night. The doctors tried to save her but they couldn't. She wasn't strong enough."

Jonas stared. For the first time since they met, he looked distant. Almost remorseful. Empathy, like rain running through cracks in cement, trickled over his face.

"And you couldn't save her either, could you? I know what you're feeling," Jonas said.

Emma expression wrenched in a cross of pain and anger.

"Who are you to tell me what I feel?" she said, tears coating her voice. "How dare you. I was adopted. Never knew my own parents. The people who took me in were the only family I had in my life and they were taken from me. Slaughtered like animals in a meat house. You couldn't know what it feels like to lose everything that meant something. To never even have the chance to say goodbye. Didn't you ever care about anyone enough Jonas to put your life on the line? To take the bullet, just because it was someone you loved. For God's sake. Didn't you ever fight for someone. That's the one thing in the world worth fighting for. Didn't you ever care enough about anyone to make a difference."

Jonas remained quiet. A warm wind fanned the stagnant air and blew back his hair. Outside, police sirens sounded.

"I have to leave now. That's the problem in life," he told her. "There's enough time."

Struggling, Emma pointed the Glock.

"I can't let you go," she said.

Jonas smiled. "Then I suppose you'll have to kill me."

Emma's finger shook on the trigger.

Turning, he walked towards the door.

Jonas!" Emma yelled.

Turning around, Jonas looked at her.

"Diggs told me about The Agency. He said I came from the same place as you. You called me to come to that Nevada prison. I need the truth." She paused, biting at her lips. "Are you my father?"

After a long silence, "Your family raised you Emma. Made you who you are. They died years ago."

"Don't toy with me." The gun shook in her hands.

Jonas turned towards the window. "You know I love this little town. It was once called Mauch Chunk, home of the sleeping bear. It's nostalgic. Full of memories. I met a boy here once. He was shy. Backward. But he was also strong. Gifted." Jonas lifted his head as if trying to remember. "Keenan. Yes. That was it. Keenan Braddock. I'm told he moved south. I'm sure I'll be paying him a visit someday. It seems that no matter how hard some people try to escape each other, everything goes full circle."

Emma stared. "Why are you telling this?"

"Because Emma." He paused. "He's your brother."

Emma's eyes widened. "I don't have a brother."

Jonas smiled. "Really? I wouldn't worry. You just found it in you to save the world. I'm sure you'll find the truth about that too."

Jonas started walking but stopped again in the dark, facing away from Emma. After a long pause he said, "Yes."

"What?"

Jonas again hesitated. "You asked me a question. I know what it's like to fight for someone, just because they're worth fighting for."

Without another word, Jonas walked out the door.

Gun shaking in her hand and a sudden warmth flooding the room, Emma passed out on the floor.

96

Heroes in the Mist

Emma floated again. She overlooked the deserted field next to the road where Diggs attacked her. Saw herself knocked out cold on the rocks. Saw Diggs standing overtop of Maddy.

"Help me sis." Maddy's pleas echoed her mind. "Please!"

Sirens blared in the distance. Diggs looked up. A fine mix of dirt and blood stained his cheek. Police were moving in. Checking secondary roads. He'd be lucky to escape.

Picking the mask up off the ground, Diggs put it back over his head. It made him feel powerful. Invincible.

"Inhuman," Diggs mumbled and crunched the handle of the knife in his fingers.

He looked down at Maddy. His dark eyes, dead pools staring from behind a white mask, were stained with ambitions of blood.

"Nobody is gonna help you here," Diggs said.

Maddy shook uncontrollably. Diggs raised the knife but stopped short. Something stirred in the woods. It wasn't loud. More like a broken branch snapping under the weight of a shoe.

Grabbing Maddy by a tuft of hair, he dragged her to her feet.

"Who's out there!" Diggs shouted. He tightened the knife under the tender edges of her chin. "You hear me? Any closer and I'll open this kid up!"

Diggs listened again. More shuffling noises. It came from in front of him, near a small embankment.

A haunting wind shook the trees. Someone emerged from the woods. Moonlight, silvery as old tombstones, shined in his dark eyes. Diggs could see a long scar, jagged as lightning, extending down the side of his cheek. A long-handled hunting knife hung from his hand and goddamn, if he wasn't smiling.

Diggs threw Maddy to the ground. He picked up his shotgun and fired off two quick rounds. The stranger veered left behind a crop of trees.

Holding the gun firm, Diggs took a step forward. He probed the darkness. Everything grew quiet again. No crickets or owls. If he didn't kill the stranger, he at least scared him off.

Craning his head around, Maddy crawled towards her sister on skinned knees.

"Where do you think you're going." Diggs reached down and dragged her back by the ankle but was again halted by noise in the woods.

Diggs turned around just as an explosion of leaves erupted at the edge of the tree line. The stranger rushed out. Spinning around, Diggs fired off another shot.

The stranger buckled. He grabbed his shoulder and staggered back by the force of the impact. Still, he refused to surrender. Regaining his balance, he stormed ahead and speared Diggs, head-first.

Diggs stumbled against the side of the car. Swinging left, he pulled the trigger but the chamber of the gun clicked emptily. Flinging the shotgun like a wooden club, he caught the unwanted visitor in the jaw.

Still, the stranger kept coming.

Diggs flung the car door open and jumped in. The stranger latched on to his shirt but Diggs wriggled free.

"Let go!" he shouted, revving the engine.

Tromping down on the gas pedal, he spun the tires in the dirt.

The ensuing moments played out like a slow-motion movie.

———

Maddy wobbled to her feet. Her nightgown, once white and clean but now covered in grime, looked ghostly in the wind against swaying wheat fields and fleeting clouds under moonlight. Her bare feet, dirty and unstable, stepped into the middle of the road. She turned her head at the loud roar of an engine. She froze; a deer caught in oncoming headlights. Her mouth opened but the scream never came out.

A loud thump sounded out. The young girl's frail body connected with the corner of the oncoming vehicle, just above the headlight. Maddy flew up on the hood. The blow was strong enough to crack the windshield, shattering it into a spider web. Finally, she rolled back down and landed in a bed of rocks and weeds.

Never easing up on the pedal, Diggs disappeared down the darkened road.

———

The night was haunted by a soft wind rustling like ghosts hidden in tall grass. Gripping his shoulder, the stranger staggered forward. He looked at Maddy. The girl's blank eyes stared up at the stars. Breath shallower than a river after a long summer drought, a tint of blue colored her cheeks.

Across the road, Emma lay twisted in the dirt. A slight groan escaped her. She fought to regain consciousness or at least escape some unforgiving nightmare.

Bending down, the stranger touched Maddy's cheek. A teardrop, no larger than a pearl, crystalized in the corner of her eye.

Picking the young girl up off the ground, he cradled her in his arms. He began to walk. How far, he didn't know. A mile. Maybe two. The bullet in his shoulder stung with the teeth of vinegar on an open wound. Still, he stumbled forward. He shielded the girl from thorns and branches as he tramped through the woods.

The stranger crossed an embankment and slogged through a stream. Hair wet and tangled, the young girl moaned as if trapped in some inescapable cage leading to the stone walls of death.

The stranger's feet grew tired and worn from a wet rain that turn the dirt to mud. Still, he pushed on. Breathing hard, he reached the top of a steep ridge. Finally, he halted. He looked down at a small trail that cut through a wooded area. Beyond that, he found what he was looking for.

97

Truckin

A steady rain began to fall. It tapped on the windshield. Eddie Tout flicked on the wipers as the eighteen-wheeler rumbled down the road. Blake Shelton belted out a country song on the radio.

Eddie drummed his fingers on the wheel. He reminisced about Monique, a French girl he met in Baltimore. After a drink at Moe's Fisherman's Wharf, they walked down by the water at Inner Harbor. He kissed her softly under the moon. By sunrise he was gone, riding the highway and crossing state lines.

A trucker's life for sure.

Fiddling with the defroster, Eddie slammed his fist on the dashboard. She was acting up again. He pulled a handkerchief out of the glove box and wiped mist off the windshield. That's when it appeared in the middle of the road.

"What the..."

Eddie slammed the brakes. Tires squealed. The monster rig came to a halt. Bright headlights beamed on a man. A dark stain, maybe blood, darkened his shirt by the shoulder. Scars knifed his cheek. Cradling a young girl in his arms, he bent down on one knee. The young girl's dark hair hung wetly, touching the tarred road.

Eddie picked up his cell and dialed 911.

"Got trouble," he told the dispatcher. "Some guy is standing on the road. It looks like he was in an accident. There's a girl with him. Unconscious or maybe..."

"What's your location, sir," the dispatcher cut in.

"Hangman's crossing on 443, about mile or so down from Walmart."

The dispatcher grew quiet. "Please stay in the car."

"What?"

"There was an incident in that area tonight."

"What do you mean, incident?"

"People were injured," the dispatcher said hesitantly. Her voice remained calm. "Police are on the way. What does the man look like?"

"A big guy. He got a long scar on his cheek. Looks like he could be bleeding near the shoulder. Maybe shot. The little girl isn't moving."

"Understood," said the dispatcher. "Do not under any circumstance approach..." her voice trailed off in static.

"You still there? Hello? Shit!" He slammed the cell phone on the dash.

The man remained kneeling in the road. Lightning streaked crossed the sky, coupled with a delayed clap of thunder. The rain grew heavier.

Illuminated in headlights, Eddie looked at the young girl's limp body. No movement at all. Her face was ashen white. If she wasn't dead, she soon would be.

Biting down on his lip, Eddie reached down and pulled a crowbar out from underneath his seat. Never knew when you'd run into some asshole at a truck stop across state lines. Gathering his courage, he opened the cab door and got out.

———

The stranger in the road stood up straight. The freaking guy was a house.

"Easy," Eddie warned. Tapping the crowbar in his hand, he again glanced at the girl dangling in the man's arms. "Help is on the way. What happened?"

The man said nothing. He walked forward, stumbling on wobbly legs.

"That's far enough!" Eddie shouted.

The man stared at him. No. Stared through him, almost as if boring a hole in his head.

"Drop it," he demanded, eyeing the crowbar in Eddie's hand.

A gush of heat singed the wet air, so much so that Eddie swore a crux of steam rose off the tarred road. He felt faint and stumbled against the side of the rig. The crowbar fell from his hand. It clanged off the blacktop.

Rain slapped the road as the man stepped towards Eddie. Reaching out, he put the young girl in the truck driver's arms.

"There's one more," he said, chest heaving as he winced with pain. "She's down the road. In the woods near a clearing."

Eddie's eyes drifted in a haze. Another distant rumble of thunder sounded in the valley. It lit up the sky over the eastern mountains.

"Who are you?" Eddie finally asked.

The man stared. "Call me Jonas."

Turning, he limped off into the darkness of night.

98

The World Rebooted

An odor of ammonia flooded Emma's nostrils. She abruptly opened her eyes. Someone had smelling salts under her nose. People with white suits and breathing apparatuses ran back and forth.

"Clear!" someone shouted.

Bending down, a man with straggly hair took off his mask and touched Emma's shoulder.

"I'm Ashton," he told her.

Emma's head turned frantically. "There's a virus…"

"We know," he cut in. "Headquarters told us everything." He looked over at Sharky. His body fermented in the warm night air. "No needle tracks and no spills on the carpet. I think you got here in time." He smiled and glanced over at Diggs's remains. "We know about Diggs. Lanster is also under arrest back at Area 51."

Eyes glazed, Emma looked around. "How did you know I was here?"

Ashton said, "We got an anonymous tip. The caller said you were knifed. Who else knew you were here?"

Emma hesitated. "Jonas Blackheart."

"Who?" Ashton asked again.

Emma paused, her mind drifting to the fears of her past.

"He's a friend," she said.

Ashton shook his head. "Nobody was here when we arrived."

Two paramedics came over and loaded Emma on a gurney. She stared ahead as they wheeled her outside. Her eyes grew heavy.

Regardless of all that happened, her thoughts floated back to that night long ago, the one that altered her life forever. Jonas was there. He tried to rescue Maddy from Diggs. He tried to save both of them. Somewhere along the road on that critical night, he looked inside Maddy's mind. Felt the terror that she was feeling. For years he lived inside a cold cellblock, little to do but dream and think. Still, he never forgot about that night. He never forgot Emma who fought so valiantly to save her sister's life.

"Jonas," she said in a whisper.

Ashton bent down. "What was that Emma?"

However, Emma began to drift. Fall away from the world. This time not with nightmares of a life gone by but in quiet solitude. She would survive. She knew that. If it was the last thing she ever did, she would survive and live to fight another day.

The End

Scene from **The 7th Jackal**, Book 1

a novel by J.L. Davis

Brave Strangers

"Ditch it!" AJ fell down in the dewy grass of Sam Miller's baseball field. Headlights from a car fleetingly passed over him and faded down the road. Sticking his head up, he gawked around. "All clear," AJ said. He crawled off his knees and began running across the field.

Becca and Keenan hurried along behind him. Just up ahead stood the brooding underbelly of Pisgah Mountain.

AJ's dog Taff led the charge. They crossed a thin reedy path at the foot of the woods. Crickets chirped all around them.

"Tugger is out there," Keenan said. "I can feel him."

Becca slipped an arm around her friend. "Don't worry. We'll find him."

AJ flicked on his flashlight. "Stay together. If you see something move, shout."

Becca shuddered. "That killer who murdered the girl on the mountain could still be around. What do we do if he finds us?"

A devilish grin played across AJ's lips. Digging into his trousers, he pulled out a surprise. "This is what we do." He eyed the shiny barrel of a .38 revolver.

"You brought a gun!" Becca drew back in fright, her knees

knocking just a bit.

"I hooked it from my grandparent's house."

"You really think it'll come to that?"

"Who knows?" AJ snapped a twig off a birch tree and stuck it in his mouth. "At least if trouble knocks we'll be ready."

He stuck the gun back in his trousers. Shaking his head smartly, he squinted like a gunslinger looking into the sights of the sun and took a deep breath. "Okay then. Let's kick some ass."

———————

Sticking their sneakers in the dirt they began the long hard climb up the mountainside. Traveling wordlessly, Keenan took the lead and lead the group by way of a sixth sense.

Hampered by a bad leg, Becca struggled to keep pace with AJ. His faithful dog Taff plodded alongside of him. More than once he reached down and rubbed the animal's head as if it were a magic lamp. With any luck it would help bring them all back home safely when the adventure finally ended.

Something in the forest made AJ abruptly stop.

"What is it?" Becca whispered.

"Up ahead on that ridge. I thought I saw something move." He spun around with the gun. Becca and Keenan ducked.

"Take it easy with that." Becca wiped sweat off her forehead. "You could kill someone."

AJ took his hand off the trigger and hoisted himself over the rotted trunk of a tree. "Relax," he said. "The safety is on."

Keenan's eyes shifted over the landscape. Struggling to see, he pointed into the misty darkness that led to a ridge cut into the mountain's highest cliff.

"That way, I think," he said.

The stars shined but were mostly hid behind the towering forest. Ripe with clusters of fat leaves, the trees rustled in the warm wind. AJ gasped when he thought he saw a large figure crouching in the shadows. He pointed his flashlight at it and exhaled.

"It's just a big rock. Scared you, didn't it?" He wiped a runner of sweat off his brow.

"Shush." Keenan stalled cold in the dirt. "Turn off your flashlight," he whispered.

The forest turned dead silent. Even the crickets stopped chirping. Cryptic as the cold breath of a killer, the only noise heard was the wind whispering in the leaves of trees. Still the most menacing sound of impending danger did not come from the murky bowels of the forest but unmistakably from one of their own.

Taff began to growl.

J.L. Davis (Jeff Davis) was born and raised in Jim Thorpe, Pennsylvania, the Gateway to the Poconos. He's the author of several novels, including the critically acclaimed 7th Jackal.

In earlier years, Davis worked as everything from a bartender to playing drums on the local circuit. Later he began a career in writing and has since released a number of bestselling novels. Currently he is working on a new book.

Stay tuned